PUFFIN BOOKS

IN DEEP WATER

Michelle Magorian's first ambition was to be an actress and after three years study at the Rose Bruford College of Speech and Drama, she went to mime school in Paris. All this time she had been secretly scribbling stories and in her mid-twenties she became interested in children's books and decided to write one herself. The result was *Goodnight Mister Tom*, a winner of the *Guardian* Award and the International Reading Association Award. Michelle now lives in London where she continues with both her acting and writing careers.

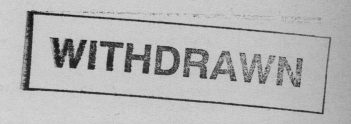

IN DEEP WATER
and Other Stories

Michelle Magorian

PUFFIN BOOKS

PUFFIN BOOKS

Published by the Penguin Group
Penguin Books Ltd, 27 Wrights Lane, London W8 5TZ, England
Penguin Books USA Inc., 375 Hudson Street, New York, New York 10014, USA
Penguin Books Australia Ltd, Ringwood, Victoria, Australia
Penguin Books Canada Ltd, 10 Alcorn Avenue, Toronto, Ontario, Canada M4V 3B2
Penguin Books (NZ) Ltd, 182–190 Wairau Road, Auckland 10, New Zealand

Penguin Books Ltd, Registered Offices: Harmondsworth, Middlesex, England

First published by Viking 1992
Published in Puffin Books 1993
3 5 7 9 10 8 6 4 2

Printed and bound in England by Clays Ltd, St Ives plc
Filmset in Bembo

For Peter, with love

Acknowledgements

Jane Murphy and Matthew Murphy (No Sweat); Steve Bailey, Sue, Jenny, and Lizzy (Head Race); The pupils at Towyn Junior CP School (Lost); Peter Venner (Sea-legs).

CONTENTS

OUT WITH THE TIDE

'He's not dead,' interrupted Josie.

She stood barelegged in the doorway, her brother Jack's voluminous white T-shirt dangling round her knees.

The young policewoman in the armchair swivelled round. Lying in her lap in some plastic sheeting was a sodden navy blue jersey with the Gynmouth ferry motif embroidered on the chest. The elbows had been darned badly. Jack's work.

'We're not saying he is,' said the young woman.

'But he's missing,' wailed Josie's mother.

Her parents were sitting on the sofa in their night-clothes. Her father looked pale.

'How much have you overheard?' he asked.

'I know his dinghy has been found in Fleet Creek and that three bodies have been washed up on a sandbank. And I know that some people on the boats moored by the pontoon outside Laura's café heard people shouting for help but couldn't do anything because the tide was too fast.'

Josie's mother was sobbing now.

'And I know he's not dead.'

A tall thin policeman emerged from the kitchen with mugs of tea on a tray.

He glanced down at Josie.

'I've made one for you too,' he said.

She took one with a nod of thanks.

'Ugh,' she said after the first sip. 'It tastes like treacle.'

'I've sugared them,' he explained.

'For shock, I suppose.'

'Josephine!' said her mother sharply.

Josie shrugged her shoulders.

'You're a hard girl.'

'Mum, he's not dead.'

'Stop saying that, will you!'

Josie looked steadily at the police.

'No one's identified him yet, have they?'

'No,' said the policeman. 'Why don't you sit down?'

Josie hesitated for a moment and then sat on the armchair nearest her father.

'That's why we came,' the policewoman explained quietly. 'We brought this jersey round . . .'

'It's Jack's,' she said.

'We know,' murmured her father.

By now her mother had begun to moan. Josie was acutely embarrassed by this display and she hated herself for feeling that way. Perhaps her mother was right. Perhaps she was hard.

'We should never have moved down here,' her mother sobbed. 'It's the biggest mistake . . .' She shook her head. 'Always in trouble that boy. Always in trouble.'

Josie's father looked up in alarm.

'Not with the police.'

'Just my mother,' Josie muttered.

'We should never have moved,' Mrs Pearce moaned. 'We should never have moved.'

Josie gripped her mug tightly, controlling a strong desire to scream 'shut up'. Her brother was missing, perhaps lying injured somewhere, but her mother still had to be the centre of attention.

'He's only seventeen. Seventeen! And I had such plans for him.'

'That jersey . . .' interrupted Josie. She hesitated.

'It was found on one of the bodies. A youth,' the policeman finished for her.

'Was he big, with hair like mine?'

'Yes,' said the woman, looking at Josie's untidy scrub of black curls.

'But it can't be him! He knows the river really well now.'

'No one knows everything about the river,' said the policeman. 'Not even people born here. The ebb-tide can sweep the most experienced people out to sea.'

'But that's why Jack wouldn't risk taking his dinghy out.'

'Normally, perhaps,' said the policeman, and then he hesitated.

'You might as well tell her,' said the policewoman.

'Tell me what?'

'The people who overheard them told us they sounded the worse for drink.'

'Jack doesn't drink,' protested Josie. 'He's had beer, but . . .'

The policeman raised his eyebrows.

'I sometimes let him drink with us at mealtimes,' said Josie's father, 'so that he can learn to drink sensibly.'

'I see.'

'You shouldn't have let him,' sobbed Josie's mother. 'I told you he'd come to a sticky end.'

Josie started to giggle nervously. 'Don't you mean a watery end, Mum? Sorry,' she said, trying to stifle a laugh.

'You see what I have to put up with?' cried her mother to the policewoman. 'Ever since she came here she's become heartless.' She began to rock backwards and forwards. 'The sooner we leave this terrible place, the better.'

Josie pulled the T-shirt over her knees and slid her legs up underneath it, so that only her feet stuck out. She stared at the pink patches between her sunburnt toes. It was their second whole summer in Gynmouth and she had never been so brown. She liked living in Gynmouth now. She didn't want to return to Birmingham with its noisy, dusty summers. Her mother would only start complaining again anyway and want to move somewhere else.

The police were staring anxiously at her mother now. It annoyed Josie to see them so taken in by her histrionics, but then Josie had seen it so many times she had grown indifferent to it.

'Dad, you're sure Jack's missing? Have you telephoned . . .'

'All the places he might have stayed? Yes.'

Josie turned her attention to the police.

'What are you doing about finding him?'

'There were only three men seen in the boat.'

'I see. So you're not even bothering to look.'

Her father sprang to his feet and slapped her face. Josie was stunned. So was her father. Full of remorse he sat on the arm of her armchair and held her.

'I'm sorry,' he said.

'It's OK, Dad,' she said, her eyes stinging.

'It's difficult for you, I know,' he began.

'It isn't difficult, Dad, because I know he's still alive.' Her voice began to waver. 'He wouldn't take any risks if he thought I might be left alone. He wouldn't do that to me.'

'You're not alone, Josie. You've got us.'

She glanced across at her mother's puffy red face, now half submerged in a handful of tissues. She *was* alone. Her father spent all his free time coping with her mother's swinging moods. Josie hated her. If she wasn't complaining about life itself, she complained about Jack. And Josie was always left to defend him.

'You're always too busy. Jack's the only person who listens to me.'

'I'm listening now.'

Her mother gave a loud howl.

But not for long, Josie thought. With her mother around there was no point in even trying.

The policewoman joined Mrs Pearce on the sofa and gingerly put an arm round her shoulders.

'We moved here to get away from muggers and drug pushers, and the rough element in his school,' sobbed Mrs Pearce. 'But there was no saving him. Instead of working for his GCSEs, all he thought about was that wretched river. He became a good-for-nothing lay-about.'

'He's not a layabout. He works hard, and stop talking about him in the past tense,' said Josie.

'He's been a bad influence on you too. You were doing well at school until this boat fever got hold of you.'

'Mum, please. Jack's missing. We've got to find him. He might be lying somewhere unconscious.'

'Well he's only brought it on himself.'

'That's enough,' said Josie's father quickly.

'Oh. Taking sides now, are you?'

At this juncture Josie's father usually gave a resigned shrug and walked out of the room. To her surprise, he stayed.

'If I have to,' he said wearily.

'I'm afraid we need you to come with us,' began the policeman awkwardly.

Mr Pearce nodded and stood up. 'Yes, of course.'

There was a loud knock at the front door.

'Are you expecting anyone?' asked the policeman.

Josie leapt from the armchair.

Outside the front door, in an old faded fishing smock and jeans, stood Bill Adams. Bearded and permanently brick-coloured, he idolized Jack as much as Josie did.

He flung his huge arms around her and crushed her with such ferocity she thought her ribs would break. When he released her, she could see his eyes were brimming.

'It's not him,' he said, smiling. 'It's not him.'

There were only the four of them in the living-room now. The police had left.

Josie had put on some jeans and one of Jack's sweaters. Although it was a balmy night, tiredness had made her feel cold.

Her father passed round a tin of biscuits.

It was strange seeing the two men sitting opposite one another, her dad so pale and clean shaven with his bald patch, and Bill Adams so hairy and darned-looking.

'I hope you didn't mind me identifyin' the youth, Mr Pearce,' he began hesitantly, 'but I was near, and when the police discovered I knew Jack . . .'

'I'm glad you did. And call me Greg.'

Bill nodded. He looked relieved.

'I know how fond of you Jack is,' added Greg Pearce. 'He's always talking about you.'

'He's a good lad. Keen.'

'You don't have to be kind about him. We know what he's like,' snapped Mrs Pearce.

Bill looked surprised.

'Oh yes,' she continued. 'You don't know the half of it.'

'Please, Mum,' said Josie.

She could see Bill was embarrassed.

'If we'd known he'd wanted to work on the ferries permanently, we'd never have let him start in the first place. We thought it was just a holiday job.'

'He's got another year of school,' pointed out her father. 'A lot can happen between now and then.'

'Every night he comes home late. We never know where he is.'

'You do!' said Josie, exasperated. 'He's on the ferry.'

'Causing trouble, I expect.'

'Collecting money.'

'Boy with a brain, collecting money! He just does it to annoy me.'

'I suppose he's gone missing just to annoy you too.'

'I wouldn't be surprised.' She blew her nose. 'He can stay in at night from now on.'

Bill cleared his throat.

'Mrs Pearce, I don't want to upset you any more than I have to, but if he hasn't turned up by midday . . . ' He stopped. 'What I'm sayin' is . . .' He lifted his hands awkwardly.

'You haven't given up hope?' protested Josie.

'No. But we've got to be realistic.'

'Couldn't we go and search the bank on the other side of the river?'

Bill nodded. 'But we'll wait till the tide comes back in.'

'In case he's washed back in from the sea?' asked Josie quietly.

'Yes.'

'I still think he's ashore. He could have been locked up somewhere by accident. What about the public lavatories near the slip-slide?'

'Kept open all night.'

'Someone's boat-house?'

'That's a possibility. But most of the boat-houses are further down the river. What would he be doin' there? No. Between the time he left me and now, he's just disappeared. It ent like him.'

There was something different about the room, thought Josie. And then she realized it was quieter. Her mother had stopped crying. Instead she was staring at Bill, gripping her tissues.

'Can't we do anything?' whispered Josie.

'Not really. The coastguards'll be keepin' a look-out and the police will start searchin' for him if he hasn't turned up by midday. Sittin' near the phone's probably the best thing you can do, Josie.' He glanced at her father. 'But I'm goin' to look along the stretch of river on the other side.'

'I'll come with you,' said Greg Pearce.

'What about me?' blurted out Josie's mother. 'No one seems to be thinking about me. That boy has worn my nerves down. He's wrecked our lives. If it hadn't been for him we would never have moved here.'

Josie was astounded. It had been her mother's idea to move. She and Jack had begged to stay put. Not only had they been forced to leave their school and their friends, but her father had given up a good job. All for her mother's nerves.

It had all started on a day trip to Gynmouth. From the moment her mother had seen the pastel-coloured houses clustered together across the river she had fallen in love with the place. Once in Gynmouth she declared, all her problems would be solved.

They weren't of course. She just complained about different ones.

'I had to leave all my friends,' she said bitterly.

What friends? thought Josie. She had snubbed or worn down so many people in Birmingham she didn't have any left.

'And it's so difficult to make new ones here.'

'It always takes a bit of time for new-comers,' said Bill.

'Mr Adams is right, we've not been here very long,' said Josie's father. 'You'll make friends soon.'

'Not once they know I've a son like mine.'

'That's rubbish,' said Josie.

'Don't be rude to your mother,' warned her dad.

'He's good and kind,' she muttered.

And he's always there when I need him, she thought. And she often needed him, badly. She wouldn't be able to cope with anything if Jack wasn't around.

'I'm finished,' wailed Mrs Pearce. 'I can't go on. I just can't go on.'

They stared at her awkwardly while she began swaying and weeping again.

'Shall I make us some tea?' said Bill suddenly.

'Yes, please,' said Josie's father.

'I'll come and help you,' added Josie.

While she and Bill pottered about the kitchen, Josie's father took her mother upstairs to bed.

The washing-up bowl was stacked with unwashed mugs. Bill filled the kettle while Josie rinsed out three of them.

'Your mother and Jack certainly don't hit it off, do they?'

'No.'

'What seems to be the problem? Untidy room? Doesn't help with chores? Girlfriends ring up all hours?'

'No. Lack of ambition, my mother says. She wants him to be a big business man. Or a lawyer. Or a bank manager. Whatever it is, she'd like him to wear a suit.'

'I can't see Jack wearin' a suit.'

'Neither can I. He'd be miserable. He's not interested in money and things like that.'

Bill laughed.

'No. He can't be. Workin' on the ferry don't pay too well.'

'He's really pleased to be on the lower ferry.'

'I know. He's been badgerin' me to show him how to turn it round. He's quick, mark you.'

'He's the best,' said Josie.

She noticed Bill looking out of the window. The sky was beginning to grow light. The tide would be coming in soon. She felt sick.

'I've given her one of her sleeping pills,' said her father in the living-room. 'I'm sorry you had to be dragged through our family dramas, Bill.'

Bill gave a shrug and handed him a mug of tea.

'She's not been too well the last couple of years.'

'What's up with her? That is, if you don't mind me askin'.'

'Jack – it is,' said Josie.

'No. It's more than that,' said her father. 'She just feels low all the time. Can't seem to shake it off. On rare occasions she'll get enthusiastic about things but she gets over-enthusiastic, if you know what I mean, and then you know she's going to come down with a crash, but you don't know when. She was like that about moving here. Excited to the point of being feverish.' He sighed. 'Now she says she feels lonely. I wish she could make some friends down here. I'm sure that would make her feel better.'

'Has she tried joining any of the groups run by the new-comers?' asked Bill. 'There's plenty of 'em.'

'No. She loves cooking and she's excellent at it; soufflés, home-made pâtés, all that sort of thing. I thought she'd like to join the Women's Institute because of it or the Wine-Making Group. But . . .' he shrugged. 'I suppose it's all a bit tame after city life.'

'About Jack,' said Bill slowly, 'she doesn't seem too happy about him workin' on the car ferry.' He hesitated. 'Is that how you feel?'

'I minded at first, but not now. It's his life.'

'He's good to have around. Most of the lads don't have two words to say. They get bored after a while and look for better-paid jobs, or go on the dole. But he's always looking out for herons or making funny comments about the day-trippers and the cars, or looking at the river.'

There was a moment's silence. Outside they could hear the faint sounds of gulls.

'Did you recognize the person you identified?' asked Josie's father quietly.

'No. I should think he were a grockle. Same age as Jack though. Some mother's heart will be breaking today.'

'Oh, no!' said Josie suddenly. 'It's Mothering Sunday today. And I haven't bought a card. Hell! That'll be a month of Mum saying no one loves her.'

'Josie!'

'I'm sorry, Dad, but it's true.'

'I've got one in the drawer in case you both forgot.'

Relieved, Josie sank back in the armchair.

'Thanks, Dad.'

They drank their way through mug after mug of tea, watching the sky slowly growing lighter. It was all Josie could do to swallow it. By the time fresh mugs were being made, hers had gone cold, hardly touched.

Her father was about to make some toast for himself and Bill before setting out with him, when there was a light tap at the door.

'The police,' he said in alarm.

But it was Jack, flanked by two pot-bellied men in their twenties. He towered above them clutching a bucket filled with mackerel and smiled sheepishly down at them.

Josie burst into tears and flung her arms round his waist.

'Are we glad to see you,' said his father.

Jack held the buckets up triumphantly and then sagged. The two men caught him by his elbows.

'He's had a few,' commented Bill.

Josie broke away.

Jack put his finger to his lips.

'Shhh,' he said, and then promptly vomited all over the porch.

'Oh, Jack,' she cried furiously. 'How could you?'

'Let's keep our voices down,' said her father. 'We don't want to wake your mother up again.'

'Mum!' called Jack, 'I've got a Mother's Day present for you.'

'Not now, Jack,' said his father.

He and Bill caught him under the arms.

'You realize we've had the police here,' said his father, over Jack's shoulder.

The men looked alarmed.

'He said it would be all right,' said the one in the trainers and Bermuda shorts. 'When he found someone had nicked his dinghy, he decided to come with us. We were just going out on the high tide to do some night fishing.'

'We thought he'd really gone out with the tide,' said Bill.

'Pardon?' said his mate.

'Nothing,' said Bill. 'Just an expression for someone who's died.'

'Did you give him the drink?' asked Josie's father.

'It was just a bit of fun,' they said awkwardly. 'He didn't object.'

'Were you all drinkin'?' asked Bill angrily. 'Out at sea?'

'We can handle it,' said the one in trainers.

'And handle a boat at the same time?'

The men shrugged and began to back off.

'Thank you for bringing him home,' said Mr Pearce curtly.

'Ruddy grockles,' Bill muttered, watching them walking quickly down the road. 'Hire boats like they think they're on a blimmin' fairground.'

Jack was still hanging on to the mackerel with grim determination.

'Dad,' he said, 'we've got to put it in the freezer before Mum wakes up.'

'All right, Jack,' said his father.

He and Bill helped drag him into the living-room while Josie looked on in disgust.

'Make up a big jug of water and fill up one of these pint glasses,' ordered her father.

'To throw over his head?'

'For him to drink. We must get as much liquid down him as we can before he passes out.'

He and Bill lowered him on to the sofa. With great difficulty they pulled off his smock.

'Dad,' said Jack, placing his large brawny hands on his father's shoulders. 'Do you think she'll be pleased?'

'I expect so, Jack.'

Jack gave a crinkly smile and then went a yellow colour. At this moment Josie walked in with the water.

Bill and her father pushed his head between his knees. Josie slammed the water down beside them.

'Josie, put the fish in the freezer, will you?'

She snatched up the buckets.

'And Josie . . .'

'Yes?'

'I wouldn't mention this to your mother.'

'Fine,' she said sarcastically, and stormed into the kitchen.

'Oh dear!' whispered her father to Bill.

He gave Jack the pint mug but it slipped through his fingers and fell to the floor.

'I had it, Dad,' said Jack, 'I had it.'

His father held a fresh glass to Jack's mouth.

'It's so she can make her mackerel pâté,' he continued. 'It's a surprise. You really think she'll like it?'

'Of course, Jack. Now drink up.'

Josie stalked back through the room.

'Where are you going?' her father asked.

'Upstairs to get the camera. I'm going to take a photo of him, so he can see how revolting he looks.'

'You're staying here until we've cleaned him and the porch up.'

'No way.'

'I mean it, Josie. Sit down!'

Josie sat.

'Dad,' said Jack, his face crumpling. 'Is Josie cross with me?'

'No. Keep drinking.'

Josie stared angrily at the floor.

'Between you and your mother, Jack can't win,' Greg

Pearce muttered. 'Nothing he does is right in your mother's eyes. Nothing he does is wrong in yours. He's either a failure or superman. Just get off his back and let him be human, will you?'

'That's not fair,' Josie mumbled.

'Would you rather he was at the bottom of the ocean? I don't understand you. Here he is, alive and kicking, and all he gets is the cold shoulder treatment because he hasn't lived up to your high expectations. He's lucky to be here, especially having been under the wing of those two characters. I expect they think it's macho to get drunk.'

'Dad,' said Jack weakly, 'I don't feel too good.'

Bill leapt to Mr Pearce's side and caught Jack before he fell off the settee.

Josie sat watching them. She had never seen her brother look so ill and helpless. He was like a little boy. She didn't like him looking so weak. How could she lean on him now? And if she couldn't lean on him when she needed to, who could she lean on?

She watched her father and Bill Adams strip him down to his underpants and lay him face down on the sofa, a bucket by his side. His long brown legs draped off the end on to the floor. It was the best they could do. There was no way they could have carried him upstairs.

They tucked him up with the tenderness of besotted parents with a new-born baby and then Bill cooked breakfast while Josie and her father cleaned up the porch.

They ate it around Jack, who slept the sleep of the innocent, and then Bill left.

It was a while before Josie and her father could even look at one another. They sat silently, turning the mugs in their hands and staring at the floor. It was her father who spoke first.

'I haven't been much of a father lately, have I?' he said suddenly.

Josie looked up in surprise.

'It's not that, Dad. You've been . . .'

'Busy. I know.' He sighed. 'Don't expect the moon from Jack. He's kind and well-meaning but he has flaws like the rest of us. And Josie . . .'

'Yes?'

'He can't be a father to you.'

'I s'pose not,' she said slowly.

He gazed across at him. 'Poor Jack. So many people needing him to be something he isn't, when all he wants to do is hang about the river and just earn enough to get by.'

'Do you think Mum will want us to move back to Birmingham now?'

'Yes. But we're not going to. I've come to a big decision about your mother tonight.'

'You're not going to leave us, are you?' she cried.

'Of course not. It's about her illness. I thought I could help her on my own. But I was wrong. I'm afraid she needs outside help, Josie. Some sort of counselling. Quickly. For our sakes, too.'

Suddenly, Jack opened his eyes.

'Where's the mackerel, Dad?'

'In the freezer.'

He raised his head.

'You really think it'll cheer her up?'

'Yes, Jack.'

'Good.'

He collapsed back into the pillow and began to snore loudly.

'She'll be able to make enough mackerel pâté to last until next Mother's Day,' said Josie's father. 'We'll be

awash with mackerel pâté. We'll probably have mackerel
pâté sandwiches until I retire.'

They smiled at one another.

'Dad,' said Josie tentatively, 'you really mean it about
Mum?'

'Oh yes. I mean it. I want to spend more time with
you and Jack before we become strangers.'

They were interrupted by the sound of church bells.

He stood up and opened the window. Josie joined
him and they leaned out together.

'It's going to be another hot day,' he murmured.

Josie gazed past the church spire rising above the
higgledy-piggledy roof-tops. She could just make out
the faintest shimmer of the river. On the steep slope
beyond it were dozens of houses stacked one above the
other and behind them, green fields. She loved the
mixture of country and sea in Gynmouth. Where else
could you be woken up in the morning by sea-gulls *and*
sheep?

Her father put his arm round her and gave her a
squeeze. 'Just look at that sky,' he said.

As soon as she raised her eyes she began to laugh.

It was clear and blue with just the faintest wisp of
white cloud trailing high above it.

'Oh, Dad, I don't believe it,' she cried. 'It's a mackerel
sky!'

NO SWEAT

Mark walked out of the men's changing room to the big pool. At the end of the roped-off lanes, under the Charity Swimathon banner, sat men and women with clipboards. Like the attendants they were wearing red Swimathon T-shirts.

Mark stood uncertainly for a moment. He had been told his lane was the second one in from the far side. He walked alongside the pool past the white plastic chairs to where a young man was sitting.

'Are you the lap counter for the 12–14 group?' he asked.

'Yes. Which one are you?'

'Mark. Mark Stevens.'

The man ticked his name. 'Where's the rest of your team?'

'They're coming later. I'm swimming the first 100 lengths and they're sharing the next hundred between them.'

The man nodded.

No sweat, thought Mark.

Mark sat down, his towel draped round his shoulders. Not that he needed it. It was boiling. He twisted the red bathing-cap they had distributed to all the participants and gazed past the rows of flags, which had been hung above the pool, towards the clock. Nearly two. He dropped his shoulders and blew out a few breaths. Relax, he told himself.

Just then pop music began blaring out of two speakers. He shaded his eyes with his hands. Even though it was daytime the lights seemed brighter than usual, and there were more of them. He glanced across at the balloons decked out over the boarded-out baby pool. Already people were sitting there at white tables and chairs drinking tea or fruit juice.

To his surprise his stomach was already fluttering. He mustn't get too nervous. Nerves could exhaust you.

He began to take in the teams on either side of his lane. Looking at them through Jacko and Terry's eyes he couldn't help grinning.

On one side was a team of four youths between 16 and 18 years old. A short stocky man in his 40s wearing a peaked cap was giving them a pep talk, revving them up and waving a stop-watch. Mark guessed they were from a youth club. Boy scout stuff.

He, Jacko and Terry didn't need to join a club. They just got on and did things. No sweat.

Knowing that he was at least four years younger than the team of youths, Mark felt very superior. Just look at them, he thought, hanging on to the coach's every word, looking as serious as if they were entering the Olympics.

The young men began shaking their legs, warming up. Daft that they were all there at the same time, Mark thought. The ones that were third and fourth would be worn out from watching before they had begun.

He glanced at the team on the other side. He couldn't see anyone at first. And then he did.

She was an elderly woman with cropped grey hair. A wrinkly!

He smothered a laugh. He was going to be swimming next to a bunch of wrinklies! He could hear Jacko and Terry's shrieks and feel their powerful elbows crashing into his ribs with mirth.

He looked down hastily. He mustn't get an attack of laughter. He'd never get through one length if he did.

Out of the corner of his eye he watched her take off a heavy purple towelling robe and pull on her Swimathon bathing-cap. Embarrassing to go around in a swim-suit at her age.

'Attention everyone!' a voice rang out.

Mark sat up straight.

This was it.

A tall man in his 50s was addressing them. Mark knew the rules. He didn't have to hear them. He, Jacko and Terry had studied them enough in the sports-centre canteen. No sweat.

Before long he saw the man approach him.

'On your own?' he asked.

'The rest of my team are coming later.'

'He's doing a hundred,' said Mark's lap counter.

'How old are you?'

'Twelve,' nearly, he added inside his head. 'The others are fourteen.'

The man smiled. 'Good on you.'

To Mark's annoyance he felt a flush of pleasure. He shrugged off the man's remark.

'You'll notice some of the teams will be swimming very fast,' said the man. 'Don't let that bother you. Go at your own pace.'

Mark nodded.

'Hello Joan,' said the man, and he waved at the old woman next to him. 'Back again?'

So the wrinkly's name was Joan. Mark shut his ears to their conversation and looked up at the clock.

He could swim a length a minute up to about thirty lengths and then he'd begin to slow down.

Two hours, he reckoned. Two hours of swimming. Not the best way of thinking about it. He must pace himself, length by length and keep adding up how much money he could raise for the children's hospital.

Nice to think he'd be earning money by doing something he enjoyed.

'Everyone ready?' said the man in charge.

The coach on his left had his hand on the shoulder of the first youth.

'You can do it,' he was saying firmly.

'Wally,' muttered Mark. He was going to be swimming half the distance Mark was going to swim. Mark pulled on his hat and slipped off his towel.

He heard the wrinkly lower herself into the water. The rest of her team would probably be hobbling in hours later. That is if they hadn't pegged out first.

He was grinning again. Concentrate, he told himself firmly.

He stood up and slipped into the water.

To his surprise he felt tired. After only one length he was ready to get out. Perhaps breast-stroke was the wrong one to choose. But it was his best stroke. He'd never be able to do the crawl for a hundred lengths.

A high wave from the youth in the next lane sent a gallon of chlorine down Mark's throat and into his eyes. He coughed, gasping for breath. This was a disaster.

Relax, he told himself.

By the third length he'd got his wind back, but he

still felt wiped out. He'd steered to the side of the lane, away from the Olympic youth who was crawling at high speed and making waves all around him. The wrinkly was a more sedate swimmer.

It wasn't till he was ten lengths in that the tiredness dissipated. With relief he realized that he had been warming up in the water. That and shaking off his nerves. He had also worked out a steady rhythm. One that he felt would carry him to a hundred.

Now he was enjoying himself. He had started to glide. There was nothing to think about, nothing to worry about. There was just him and the water, the bright lights, the pumping music, the loud splashing and the reverberating voices of the spectators. The noise was deafening.

The first forty lengths were a doddle. It was around his forty-second length when the coach in the next lane started yelling at the youth in the water. 'You can do it! You can do it!'

The three other youths were yelling too, fit to bust. It annoyed Mark, the big deal they were making of it.

Mark couldn't see the youth's head, just a flurry of water drawing closer to the end of the lane. The coach pressed his stop-watch and the next youth lowered himself in. Within seconds the coach had a towel round the first youth's shoulders and was sending someone off to get hot chocolate like he'd climbed Mount Everest.

Mark turned and pushed off, glancing round for Jacko and Terry. No sign of them yet. Still, there was plenty of time.

It was when the second youth was being urged on to swim faster that the penny dropped. They weren't getting worked up about the number of lengths they were swimming. It was the time they were taking to swim them. They were obviously trying to win some record for speed. That's what all the excitement was about.

As Mark touched the side of the bath, his lap counter looked up. 'Twelve lengths to go,' he said.

And there was no Jacko and no Terry. They had to arrive soon otherwise Mark's hundred lengths wouldn't even be counted, and his team would be disqualified. Three months of working himself up to a hundred lengths down the tube. And would his sponsors pay up if their team hadn't done the two hundred lengths?

As he turned at the end of the pool, someone put a new tape on. The sound blasted out of the two speakers so loudly it nearly knocked him over.

As Mark headed back towards his lap counter, he realized that part of what had driven him to do a hundred lengths was the desire to impress Jacko and Terry. It was important that they knew he was as tough as them, even though they were approaching six feet and broad-shouldered with it. They had to be there to see him swim that hundred lengths. Be there to show their amazement and slap him on the back even though it stung like a burn when they did it. Then he'd be one of them. They would be a trio, not a duo and a hanger-on. He would never feel lost for words with them again and he'd be able to make jokes as brilliantly as them.

Ninety-eight lengths, two to go.

To his annoyance he felt a stab of jealousy for the team in the next lane. Not for their swimming ability, he was as good, but because they had mates rooting for every length they swam.

No one was even noticing Mark, aside from the lap counter, who he realized now wasn't allowed to flicker a face muscle.

It was then that he remembered the wrinkly. She was still swimming too. He had been so wrapped up in himself that he hadn't noticed that her team hadn't shown up either.

Mark swam slowly towards the end of the lane. His heart sinking, his fingers touched the wall.

'A hundred,' said the lap counter.

Mark rested his arms over the end.

'What are you going to do?' asked the man.

Mark had a lump in his throat the size of a fist. Do, he thought, do? Cry my bloody eyes out, that's what he felt like doing.

'Sorry, I'm afraid your hundred doesn't count,' he continued.

Mark nodded miserably.

Next to him the youths were whistling and cheering. If only they'd shut up and the music was turned down, he could think more clearly.

A refined voice pierced through his misery.

It was the wrinkly.

'What's up?' she asked.

None of your business, you old prune, he whispered angrily inside his head.

'His team hasn't turned up.'

'Can't he keep swimming till they do?'

'He's already swum a hundred.'

'I know.' She turned to him. 'I've been watching you out of the corner of my eye. You've done marvellously. Come on, keep going. You can give me moral support.'

'Where's your team?' he asked.

She pointed to herself. 'I'm my team. I'm trying for the two–hundred–lengths certificate.'

'Two hundred? But that's three miles,' and he stared at her, stunned.

'And a bit.'

'Sorry,' he added quickly, realizing his jaw was still open.

But he couldn't help himself. A wrinkly going for two hundred lengths!

She laughed.

Mark looked up at his lap counter. 'Can I?'

'Sure, if you think you can manage it.'

'They'll be here soon, I know they will. They've never let me down before. I expect they've been held up somewhere.'

The man nodded.

'Let's go,' said the woman, smiling.

And Mark, in spite of his desire to remain Mr Cool, found himself smiling back.

They pushed themselves on.

Now he really *would* need to pace himself.

He consciously relaxed his shoulders again and pushed more firmly with his legs. No, he thought, his mates had never let him down. Come to think of it, though, he'd never asked them to do anything before. But he hadn't asked them. They'd volunteered. No sweat, they had said. Fifty lengths. Dead easy.

So what had happened to them? He pictured them lying in a pool of blood on Wembley High Street, gasping out some garbled message to the ambulancemen about telling Mark they couldn't make it, but both sinking into unconsciousness before their vital message could be understood.

He touched the wall and turned.

A hundred and one.

Take it easy, he told himself. They'll be here. There's probably been a hold-up on the tube. They were always having trouble on their line. They were probably stuck somewhere, unable to ring the sports centre because the nearest phones had been vandalized. They'd be in a right stew, cursing and pacing the platform and punching walls.

A hundred and two lengths.

He blew heavily into the water. They could be ill of course. Both of them? No. Unless it was food poisoning from a take-away kebab or pizza. Yes, they were probably heaving up somewhere, unable even to keep down a teaspoon of water, struggling to get to the door, picking up their towels, all strength gone, but still determined to make it.

A hundred and three lengths.

When Mark swam his hundred and fiftieth length he knew that Jacko and Terry weren't going to make it. He turned over on to his back. His neck ached so painfully that he thought it would crack. He'd done a hundred and fifty useless lengths. Useless because in no way could he swim any further. If he could get out and have a break he might make it to two hundred, but it wouldn't count.

He was past caring now. He was so tired he could hardly breathe. He'd take a rest doing a slow back-stroke before climbing out.

Joan was still going. He had to call her Joan now. Wrinkly was the word Jacko and Terry used for anyone elderly and it didn't suit her. He glanced aside at her. She had more guts, stamina and strength than the two of them rolled together. He pictured them making their comments in their trendy jeans and latest trainers and jackets. Legs just that little too far apart, macho men. Hey, Marko, we forgot. He could hear them saying it. No hard feelings, eh? Slam of hand on shoulder. You know how it is? Yeah, thought Mark. I know how it is. Next year, eh? Yeah, next year, or the year after.

He smiled bitterly. His so-called mates had never intended coming at all. Oh yeah, we can do this. Oh yeah, we can do that. No sweat.

And that summed them up. No sweat. They were incapable of producing a drop of it because they didn't do anything. They were all talk.

Yet he had longed to be one of them. Longed to stop feeling tongue-tied and small and boring. But it wasn't him that was boring. He had just been bored in their company. Bored, bored, bored.

A hundred and fifty-one.

Why hadn't he seen through them before? How come he had believed all their blether? As he lay on his back, a new emotion swept through him. Anger. Anger at them. And anger with himself. As soon as he touched the wall he turned over and began to crawl. He still knew he wouldn't make it, but at least moving his neck from side to side would ease the pain. He lashed out furiously into the water like a tiger released from captivity. Wild and powerful, yet still in control. Still graceful.

As he crawled length after length he swam out all the feelings he had kept bottled up inside him for months. All the doubts he had ignored when Jacko and Terry never turned up for a practise with him, but told him they were practising on other days. How could he have been so stupid? Because he was desperate to have friends. Any friends.

Almost the dullest in his class, but not quite. Never feeling he could mix with the dumbos or the ones that got by. Switched off and switched out. That was him.

A hundred and seventy lengths.

The team beside him had finished. They were jubilant. Well-pleased with themselves.

Joan was still swimming. As if she sensed him looking at her she beamed at him. 'Think I'll make it?' she yelled.

'Yeah, 'course you will.' He nearly said, no sweat, but stopped himself.

His neck had eased up now. His shoulders and ankles ached instead. He rolled over into the back-stroke again to give himself another rest.

By the time Mark completed his one hundred and eightieth length there was no one left in the pool except him and Joan. The only people around the pool were their two lap counters and a life-guard on a high-seated podium at the side.

The man who was in charge came out of the office and gazed in Mark's direction.

Don't say he's going to disqualify me now, thought Mark. But the man grinned and raised two thumbs. He was rooting for him! He gave Joan the same message.

It was then that Mark noticed that the life-guard was smiling. Mark hadn't even bothered to look at him. And he gave a thumbs-up sign too! Three people wanted him to make it. It pushed him to complete the next length.

Soon after this incident, attendants came out of the office, curious to watch Joan and him. They appeared relaxed and not at all bothered at having to stay behind.

The early evening sun had found its way to a long window at the side and it streamed into the pool. Someone had turned the music off. It was so quiet that Mark could hear the water lapping around him. He could have been swimming in a private pool in Malibu.

Two attendants were removing the flags above their heads.

'Take your time,' said his lap counter, picking up Mark's anxiety. 'Keep to your own steady pace, we're not in a hurry.'

Ten lengths to go and he knew. He knew he was going to make it.

Please don't let me pass out, get cramp or die, he told himself.

Attendants had begun to gather round his lap counter who was now fighting down a smile.

'Come on, you're nearly there,' shouted a tall blond-haired girl.

Mark nearly choked. Jacko and Terry had been lusting after her for weeks. They never said hello to her of course. They just stared at her and talked about her. And here she was rooting for him, twelve years old, nearly, and puny. Correction, he told himself. Puny people don't swim a hundred and ninety-two lengths. Three miles!

He laughed. He had no friends and he was laughing. Crazy. But he decided he'd rather be himself and have no friends than try and pretend to be someone he wasn't. And it made him feel feather-light.

It was the last length and it was so sweet he didn't want to rush it. Joan knew and she cheered from the water. And then everyone round the pool was clapping. And the man in charge was clasping his hands above his head.

Mark came in on a leisured crawl, touched the side and hung there, high. He swam to the steps at the side. He was too weak to pull himself out of the pool from the water. He had hardly reached the chairs when his legs buckled. He sat down quickly and wrapped the towel around his aching shoulders. His legs were shaking.

His ankles ached and his feet felt as though someone had stuck them in a fridge. All he wanted to do was collapse into bed and sleep.

'Two hundred lengths,' said his lap counter, smiling.

Mark nodded, still trying to catch his breath. The man in charge grinned down at him.

'Looks like you didn't need your team-mates after all.'

'Yeah,' he agreed.

The man handed him an orange juice. Mark held it for a moment and then sipped it slowly. He wanted to sit still and take in what he had achieved. 'Two hundred lengths,' he whispered. 'I have just swum two hundred lengths.' He had proved something to himself. He wasn't sure what, but it felt very good.

'You'd best get dressed before you get too cold,' said the lap counter.

'Not yet,' said Mark, putting down the beaker.

'It's over now.'

'Not for Joan it isn't.' And he pulled himself shakily to his feet, stumbled over to her lane and started yelling.

IN DEEP WATER

'You're absolutely sure?'

'Positive. We never see him till the spring. He leaves it here all winter.'

They were standing on the jetty, hunched up in wind-cheaters and scarves, Ruth with her frizzy black hair and Maggie with her blonde fringe sticking out of woolly hats.

It was bitterly cold. The tide was out. If they had wanted to they could have walked to the boat from the shore by squelching through the mud. But there was no need. The fibreglass motor boat was tied to a small wooden jetty.

'Shall we then?'

Ruth nodded.

They glanced swiftly from side to side to check that no one was walking along the narrow dirt-track which wound its way round the creek, and then to the trees on the island.

It was really a bank, but it looked as though it could be an island, so they had called it one.

They climbed down from the jetty into the cockpit and sat in the boat as if they owned it.

A section of wood was padlocked half-way down the

doorway. They peered in over it. It was very plain inside.

There was a corner at the end to stow gear, and two seats like long benches just big enough for two people to lie down in a sleeping-bag.

'Shall we?' asked Maggie.

'Yes,' said Ruth, reading her thoughts.

Maggie hauled herself up and squeezed through head first. She gave a yell.

'Head first is not a good idea. Help, I'm stuck.'

Ruth pulled her out.

Feet first didn't work either. Maggie returned to her former burglar position and emptied herself squealing into the cabin.

'Here,' said Ruth, passing her wind-cheater and scarf through to her and she fell in soon after.

'This is ace,' said Maggie, sitting on a bunk.

Through the portholes they could see the trees on the island.

'What's he like?' she asked.

'Who?'

'The man who owns this boat.'

'I don't know, I've never spoken to him. He's never spoken to me.'

'What does he look like?'

'Ordinary.'

'Don't you ever spy on him?'

'No.'

'Shall we? This summer?'

'If you want. You won't see much. There are more interesting people down here to spy on. Especially the big house at the end of the creek. They have all sorts of posh people staying and they sit in the garden and talk. You can watch them through the trees overlooking the garden. I've never been spotted yet.'

'You are lucky,' sighed Maggie. 'All I have to spy on is traffic.'

'And cinemas, and an ice-skating rink, and the fair,' Ruth pointed out.

'I suppose so.' She smiled. 'Hey, why don't we eat in here tonight?'

'I think cooking here might be a bit dodgy.'

'I mean still cook in the tent as we planned and then bring the food over. How about it? I've never eaten in a boat before.'

'Yes. The tide'll be in. It should really rock about then.'

They heard the faint sounds of a gong being beaten.

'Lunch,' said Ruth. 'Quick. If we take too long she might start asking questions.'

They scrambled out of the boat, ran up the jetty and along the track to the end of Ruth's garden where Maggie's tent was pitched.

It was six feet high. Maggie had hauled it on the long ferry and bus journey from home to Ruth's place. When Ruth had met her at the bus-stop she had gawped at the sight of the huge kit-bag in Maggie's arms.

'You're only staying the night,' she said. 'What have you got in there, elephant pyjamas?'

Maggie had laughed and turned round to show Ruth a small second-hand haversack dangling from her shoulders.

'That's my stuff,' she said. 'This is the tent.'

'Great. I didn't think you'd bring it till the summer.'

'I couldn't wait. It's taken me this long to be allowed to stay one night. This might be my ration for the year.'

As soon as Maggie had dumped her bag in Ruth's bedroom and they had pulled on wellies in the outer porch at the back of the house, they hauled the tent down to the bottom of the garden.

'I think it's an old boy scout one,' said Maggie. 'My father got it at an auction. You have to slot these together,' she added, waving some wooden poles with metal ends.

They slotted the ridge-poles across the top of the front and back poles. After that it was a juggling act between each other and mountains of heaving canvas.

Now it was pegged out in all its khaki glory.

They pushed aside the front flaps and walked inside.

'It's great to be able to stand in a tent,' said Ruth. 'I hope you can stay again. We could sleep out here in the summer.'

Maggie raised both hands and crossed her fingers.

'I might even have a groundsheet by then.'

They left the tent and tied the door behind them. Maggie gazed out at the muddy creek.

'I still think you're lucky,' she said.

'But you're as close as I am to the sea.'

'Yes, but I'm still not allowed anywhere near it unless my parents come with me, and they never want to go.'

'It's a pity our school doesn't teach swimming. You'd think that if your parents were so scared of you drowning they'd have chosen a school which did.'

'They chose it partly because it didn't.'

The gong sounded again, only more frantically.

'Come on,' said Ruth. They ran up the garden. 'Did you bring the sausages?' she panted over her shoulder.

'Loads of them.'

Maggie was woken up by the muffled sound of Ruth's alarm clock under her bedding. Midnight. It seemed that she had only just fallen asleep.

'Maggie,' whispered Ruth. 'Wake up!'

'I am awake.' And I wish I wasn't, she thought. Having a midnight feast just now had lost its appeal. She poked her head out from under the warm covers and met an icy blast of air. In the darkness she could make out Ruth pulling on her jeans and two woollen jumpers. She couldn't back out now. Her teeth chattering, she slid out of bed and threw her trousers and jerseys over her pyjamas. She couldn't bring herself to take them off.

'Ready?' whispered Ruth.

Maggie nodded and picked up her haversack. They crept through the door and on to the landing.

Once in the porch pulling on their wellingtons and outer clothing, their exhilaration at making it that far without waking anyone took away their tiredness. They wound their scarves several times around their necks, grinned at one another and unlocked the porch door.

Outside, the moon hung brilliantly over a high tide.

They crept cautiously along the frosted grass until they were sure they were out of sight of the house and then ran alongside the high hedge towards the tent.

They stood outside it for a while, stamping their feet.

'I think it's going to snow,' commented Ruth.

'It'll cover our tracks on the jetty if it does,' said Maggie.

Inside the tent Ruth held the torch whilst Maggie poured methylated spirit into a little tin. She placed the top on, lit it and turned it up.

'Now for the sausages.'

'How many have you got?' asked Ruth.

'Twenty-four. They were a special offer. I got thin ones and thick ones.'

'Goodo.'

They each stuck a sausage at the end of a fork and held it over the flames.

'This is the life, eh,' commented Maggie, a cloud of warm breath billowing from her mouth.

The sausages took longer to cook than they had anticipated. While they were waiting, they slowly ate their way through the chocolate they had brought.

'Right,' said Maggie, waving one of the sausages. 'They look sort of cooked.'

They bit into them.

'Are you sure they're supposed to be this squishy?' asked Ruth, tugging at hers with her teeth.

'Mm,' said Maggie doubtfully. 'Mine's warm, but a bit raw. Let's hold them nearer the flames.'

'Mine's just exploded,' said Ruth. 'I think that's a good sign.'

'Maybe food always tastes a bit like this when it's cooked outside,' said Maggie.

Once cooked, they wrapped up twelve sausages and began to eat the rest. Maggie's stomach began to feel a bit weighty.

'I expect the fresh air will make us hungry again,' she said.

'I expect so,' said Ruth.

Maggie turned down the stove and untied the flaps.

'Quick,' she said urgently, 'turn off your torch.'

'What?' said Ruth.

'Turn it off!' She thrust her hand over it so that the blood showed pink through her fingers. It reminded her of the sausages, which made her feel a bit queasy so she was relieved when it was off.

'Why?' said Ruth, in the darkness.

'There's a light on in the boat!'

'Blast!' said Maggie, tearing into another sausage. 'My one night here and he has to come back.'

'Never mind,' said Ruth. 'It's a bit odd though. He's

never come down in the winter before and when he does I usually see him pottering around in the day.'

'You don't suppose . . .' said Maggie slowly. 'No, I've been reading too much Enid Blyton.'

'Go on.'

'I was just thinking, I suppose it *is* him.'

'Who else could it be?'

'Thieves.'

'Here?'

'No. I didn't think it could be.'

But Ruth was frowning. 'There's one way we can find out.'

'How?'

'If it's him he'll have a key to unpadlock that piece of wood. If it isn't it'll be broken.'

'A thief could squeeze in over the top like we did.'

'Not unless he was a midget,' said Ruth.

They bundled up the remaining sausages and poked their heads outside.

Drifting from the sky were flakes of light snow.

'If they are thieves, they couldn't have picked a worse night. A full moon and enough stars to light up a rock concert.'

'And us,' added Ruth. 'We must stop talking from now on. The water will carry even a whisper.'

Maggie gave a thumbs up.

They dashed from the tent to the high hedge and peered round to the dirt-track. The boat was still moored about a hundred yards up. A faint light glowed through the portholes.

They gave a nod towards one another and ran stealthily towards the jetty. No sooner had they stepped on to the rickety planks than it gave a loud creak. They froze. Nothing happened.

Slowly they edged their way towards the end where the boat was bobbing on the water.

Hanging across the doorway was a piece of canvas. The door had been removed. It looked as if Mr Ordinary had come back after all.

They were about to leave when Maggie gripped Ruth's arm so hard she nearly yelled. Ruth stared at her, puzzled. Maggie was pointing frantically into the cockpit and then Ruth saw it . . . the door.

The crowbar which had prized the lock away was still lying beside the broken wood. They stared at one another, alarmed.

Any minute now the canvas could be thrust aside and they would be exposed. Maggie pointed towards the rope and made a movement with her hands.

Ruth knelt down and began untying it. Maggie kept watch.

It took a long time. Her gloves off, Ruth's hands were so frozen she could hardly move them, and the rope was stiff from being knotted for months. And then it was done. She lowered the rope slowly into the cockpit.

Maggie grabbed her arm again.

'Don't do that,' Ruth mouthed.

Low voices could be heard along the dirt-track. Male voices.

They ran swiftly along the jetty.

They were bound to be seen now. The moonlight was so bright they'd be spotted before they could reach Ruth's garden.

Ruth waved frantically at some dinghies which had been pulled up and were lying on some nearby grass.

They sprinted towards them, climbed in one which had a tarpaulin, threw themselves into it and lay down pulling the tarpaulin over them.

The voices were definitely coming in their direction. They peered over the edge of the dinghy.

The motor boat didn't look as though it had moved at all. Whoever was coming down the dirt-track would be able to tie it back to the jetty with no difficulty.

Glancing aside they could make out the outline of two men carrying a large outboard motor and a can between them.

Maggie clutched Ruth's arm.

'What?' she mouthed.

'Look.'

Gradually, imperceptibly, the motor boat was beginning to drift from its mooring.

They pulled themselves down out of sight and lay with their fingers crossed, willing the boat to drift far enough away and then at least one of the thieves would be trapped on board.

The men sounded pleased with themselves. They muttered something about Calais.

'Nice job. Nice pleasant little trip,' one of them said.

And they laughed.

'Keep your voice down, Mac,' said the other.

'Who's goin' to hear us? The birds?'

'Don't mention that word. It 'as nasty connotations.'

'What?'

'Bird. Doing . . .'

'Yeah, yeah. I got it. Stop a minute will you, I wanna get me breath back.'

'You're getting flabby, Jo-Jo. You wanna come down Marco's with me, have a good work-out.'

'Mebbe.'

'Too much eating that French stuff and drinking fancy plonk.'

'It helps me think.'

'Yeah?'

They laughed.

'Come on, nearly there.'

This was followed by much grunting and then there was silence.

'Tide's moved the boat away from the jetty,' said the man called Mac.

'No problem,' said Jo-Jo. 'We just pull on the rope.'

'What rope?'

'The rope that's tied to the . . .' He stopped. 'Wait a minute. Where is it?'

'You tell me.'

They heard the heavy thump of the outboard motor being dumped on to the jetty. This was followed by footsteps hitting the plank.

'Did you untie that?' yelled Jo-Jo.

' 'Course I didn't. I leave all the boat stuff to you. You know I do.'

'We've got to get it back. It's more than my life's worth . . .' his voice tailed off.

'Could we swim after it?' suggested Mac.

'In this? We'd be dead from exposure in minutes.'

'We could row after it in one of them dinghies.'

Ruth and Maggie stared at each other in horror.

'I can't row,' said Jo-Jo. 'Can't you use the motor on it.'

'Not one that size, dip-head. It'd sink it.'

'Our one chance is the tide. With any luck it'll drift across the bank over there.'

'He must be pointing to the island,' whispered Maggie.

'Meanwhile,' he continued, 'I'm going to find out who untied the rope.'

'What d'you mean?'

'That rope couldn't have untied itself. Someone's messing us about. And they can't be too far away either.'

Ruth and Maggie held their breath.

'Ours aren't the only footprints on this jetty. We'll have to move fast before the snow covers the rest.'

'What about the boat?' asked Mac.

'Stay here and watch it. If it hits the opposite bank or you see anyone, yell out.'

'Won't someone hear us?'

'Do a bird, or something. Sorry. An owl. Use yer 'ead.'

Ruth and Maggie heard the footsteps getting closer.

According to the luminous hands on Ruth's wristwatch they stayed hidden in the boat for half an hour, but it seemed like twelve.

Jo-Jo returned, cursing and swearing. It appeared that the tide was sweeping the motor boat seawards. They spoke in low tones.

Ruth and Maggie could only make out the odd word here and there and then they heard something which made their hair stand on end.

The men mentioned an auntie who was wrapped round the stash. They weren't just thieves, they were murderers!

What if they spotted the tent and put two and two together? What if they spied on the house day after day waiting to get their revenge?

At last the men decided to leave, but it wasn't until their voices were almost out of hearing that Ruth and Maggie crawled out of the dinghy, stiff with cold and crippled with pins and needles.

They pinned themselves far back on the track and moved slowly towards the high hedge which hid the tent.

As soon as it was within reach, they flung themselves around it and stumbled up the garden, putting as much distance between themselves and the creek as fast as they could without falling over.

They crouched in the porch panting, still expecting to see Mac and Jo-Jo staring at them through the window.

'Now what?' said Ruth.

'We'll have to phone the police,' whispered Maggie.

'They'll never believe us.'

'Why not?'

'Two kids ring up in the middle of the night. They'd only ask what we were doing out of bed.'

'You're right. And if my parents find out I'll never be able to stay here again.'

They sat at the kitchen table, thawing by the range. Ruth's mother liked cooking the old-fashioned way.

'Ruth, we'll have to phone them. What about the old lady, the aunt?'

'I'd forgotten about her. She might still be alive.'

'Why would they want to take her to France?'

'To dispose of her body in a place no one would think of looking?' suggested Maggie. The thought made them shiver.

'Who's going to phone?' asked Ruth.

They decided that Maggie should phone because she could put on different voices. The telephone was in the sitting-room. With painstaking stealth they made their way across the hall and stood by it, half afraid to touch it in case it burnt their fingers.

'9–9–9,' whispered Maggie as she dialled.

'Which service do you require?'

'Police,' said Maggie in a low voice.

'Where are you phoning from?'

Maggie put her hand on the mouthpiece. 'She wants to know where I'm phoning from?'

'Just say Hurling Island.'

'Hurling Island,' said Maggie, even more huskily.

'I'll put you through.'

'This is Hurling Island Police Station,' said a male voice.

'There's been a murder,' began Maggie, panicking. 'We overheard the murderers talking and . . .'

'Steady on, slow down,' said the voice at the other end.

'But we untied their boat. Well, it wasn't their boat. It was Mr Ordinary's boat. Mr Ordinary is not his real name. I don't know his real name.'

'Let's start again, shall we?'

'All right. Only there's not much time. There's a dead aunt in the boat wrapped round the stash. And the boat is a motor boat. Only it doesn't have a motor because we untied the rope before the crooks could get the motor on.'

'Name?' said the male voice.

'Mac and Jo-Jo.'

'Which one would you like to be called tonight?' said the man, sounding distinctly weary.

'Not my name. Their names.'

'Well now. Shall we start with your name first.'

'My name?' said Maggie aghast.

'Yes.'

'Er, Fred.'

As soon as she said it she knew it was a mistake.

'Do I take it *Fred* that you have untied a motor boat and are now having pangs of conscience?'

'What else could we do? We had to stop them somehow.'

'Where are you calling from, sonny?'

'Hurling Island.'

There was a sigh.

'I know it's Hurling Island. *Where* in Hurling Island?'

'The creek,' mouthed Ruth.

'The creek.'

There were footsteps on the landing.

They froze.

'Hello,' said the voice. 'Hello. Can you give me your number?'

'I can't talk any more. Goodbye.'

They waited for the footsteps to descend, but instead there was a loud flush of the lavatory and the footsteps returned to the bedroom of Ruth's parents.

They crept up the side of the stairs, pressing themselves flat against the wall.

As soon as they reached the safety of Ruth's bedroom they tore off their clothes and threw themselves into bed.

'Made it,' groaned Maggie.

'Do you think they believed you?' whispered Ruth.

'I don't know.'

'I wonder if Mac and Jo-Jo are still looking for the boat?'

'Or us,' added Maggie, ominously.

'I'm just beginning to feel my toes again,' said Ruth sleepily.

'Me too.'

There was a pause.

'Maggie?'

'Mm.'

'Those sausages.'

'Yes.'

'You said they were a special offer.'

'Yes,' said Maggie slowly.

'They were terrible, weren't they?'

'Foul. My stomach feels as though an elephant's sitting in it.'

'My stomach feels like an elephant's dancing in it.'

'You know people who work in a chocolate factory are given loads of chocolate to put them off it, so they won't steal any of it?'

'Yes.'

'Do you think it's the same in a sausage factory?'

'Might be.'

'I don't think I'll ever eat sausages again.'

'Me neither.'

'I'd die first.'

'Night.'

'Night.'

They stared at each other's white faces over the corn-flakes. Ruth's father was cracking jokes. They were terrible jokes, but Maggie forced herself to smile because she thought it was nice that he made the attempt.

'Up talking late, I see,' Ruth's mother had said when they presented themselves for breakfast.

But it didn't seem to bother her.

Maggie watched her come in and out of sight through the hatchway which was between the kitchen and the dining-room.

'That's funny,' she said.

'Thank you, dear,' said Mr Rogers. 'You don't think my jokes usually are. Which one do you mean? I shall have to use it again.'

'Not your joke.'

'Oh. Shame.'

'There's a couple of policemen at the bottom of the garden, looking at Maggie's tent.'

'Come to make sure no one is loitering with intent, I expect.' And he grinned expectantly.

Maggie was trying to smile, but her lips had become so tight that she was sure they were stretched across her teeth in a grimace.

She glanced quickly down at the cornflakes which seemed to be swimming up at her. She was not feeling very hungry and the state of her stomach had not improved.

'They're walking up to the house,' said Mrs Rogers.

'Don't worry, Maggie,' said Mr Rogers, twinkling at her through his owlish spectacles. 'I don't think you need a licence to put up a tent.'

Maggie and Ruth stared transfixed at each other listening to Mrs Rogers open the porch door. 'Can I help?' she called.

'I hope so, madam.'

Mr Rogers, unable to contain his curiosity, left the table and headed for the kitchen.

Within seconds they could see him and Mrs Rogers and two uniformed officers through the hatchway.

They kept their heads down.

'Fred?' Mrs Rogers was repeating. 'No I don't know a boy by that name round here. Do you, dear?'

'Doesn't ring a bell.'

'Ah,' said one of them. 'I see you have youngsters of your own. Mind if I . . .'

'Of course not.'

A tall young officer with a blond moustache leaned through the hatchway. They'd seen him in the Hurling Island amateur dramatics group. He was the only policeman on Hurling Island who had a moustache.

'Know anyone called Fred?' he said grinning.

'No,' said Maggie and Ruth in unison.

'Pity. I'm sure he could give us some vital information.'

The other policeman poked his head through the hatch now.

'Whose tent is that?' he asked.

Maggie couldn't speak. Instead she pointed to herself.

'Why don't you two sit down in there and I'll bring you some tea,' said Mrs Rogers. 'You won't mind watching them eat breakfast will you?'

'Not at all, not at all.'

Before Ruth and Maggie could say, 'Let's get the hell out of here,' the two policemen were sitting on either side of Mr Rogers and looking at the girls as if they were at a tennis match. And they knew their faces were as red as beetroots. They listened in a state of high tension as the policemen chatted with Mrs Rogers about the weather and what a nice cup of tea she had made. And then Mrs Rogers returned to the kitchen to cook breakfast. The one with a moustache turned to Maggie.

'Do you think this Fred could have used your tent last night?'

'I don't know. We haven't been down there this morning yet.'

'Only, if this Fred had done, he could have seen who untied the motor boat.'

'Ruth wouldn't do anything like that,' said Mr Rogers.

'I'm sure she wouldn't. But this Fred might have and this Fred might have had good reason to.'

By now she thought she must resemble a volcano.

'Is the central heating a bit hot for you?' said Mr Rogers, noticing.

'No, Mr Rogers.'

'Thanks to this Fred, we've found the boat. It was

filled with antiques from the big house at the end of the creek. The owners are delighted.'

'Good,' said Maggie casually.

Why, she thought, didn't he look at Ruth? Because, she noted, the other one was doing that.

'Yes. Lots of antiques, bound for . . .' he shrugged.

'Calais, I should think,' put in Maggie.

'Oh?'

'Yes. I mean . . . probably.'

'So it was filled with antiques?' asked Ruth.

'Yes.'

'Just antiques?' added Maggie.

'Yes,' said the other policeman.

'No dead aunt,' said the one next to Maggie pointedly. 'Now,' he added. 'Which one of you is Fred?'

The game was up and it was a relief to pour it all out.

As the policemen took notes they nodded at intervals as if they already knew some of what Ruth and Maggie were telling them.

'Why Calais?' interrupted Mr Rogers.

'To take them to an antique market somewhere in France. Almost impossible to trace after that.'

'Marco's,' said Ruth.

'What?' said the second policeman.

'The one called Mac said he worked out at Marco's.'

'Marco's gym,' said the two policemen.

'Is that useful?'

'Very.'

'Now, about the aunt?'

'We heard them talking about her. Something about wrapping her round something.'

'She sounded Spanish,' added Ruth. 'Maracus or something.'

'No. Macares.'

'Macassa.'

At that Mr Rogers started rocking with laughter.

'Oh very droll!' he said, his glasses steaming. 'Now that's a good one.'

Everyone stared at him. Mrs Rogers peered through the hatch.

'Could you share it with us, dear,' she pleaded.

'Antimacassar,' he yelled.

'That's her,' said the girls.

'They're like huge lacy doilies,' he explained. 'You cover sofas, tables, that sort of thing with them. Some of them are quite lovely.'

'That's that then.'

'Do my parents have to know about this?' asked Maggie suddenly.

The policeman next to her looked surprised. 'Don't you want them to? They'd be very proud of you I would have thought.'

'Although you mustn't make a habit of untying boats,' added the other.

'They'd never let me stay here again if they knew I was anywhere near the creek.'

'Ah,' said Mr Rogers, his face lighting up again. 'You mean you'd be in deep water if they knew you were anywhere near deep water.'

'Exactly,' said Maggie.

But Mr Rogers was too busy chuckling to hear.

'I shall need you to make a statement,' said the policeman with the moustache.

'After they've had breakfast,' said Mrs Rogers.

'Yes, of course. No hurry.'

It was while Mr Rogers was escorting the two policemen into the sitting-room that Maggie and Ruth noticed the smell coming from the kitchen.

'Now you two,' said Mrs Rogers, beaming through the hatchway. 'You must be starving; you deserve a heroines' breakfast, so I've cooked you your favourite, Ruth. I know it's your favourite too Maggie, Ruth told me.'

She slid two plates through to them. Stacked high on top of a mound of baked beans were some extremely familiar objects.

'Sausages,' said the girls weakly.

'Yes. Tuck in. I've cooked plenty more for you to eat. I've got masses. They were a special offer.'

HEAD RACE

'You stupid berk, they're going to get past us!'

'I told you we should have had a girl cox,' said the Number Four, exasperated. 'They think more quickly.'

'I don't believe this,' moaned the Number Two, looking over his shoulder as another eight whisked easily past them.

'We should be in that current!' yelled the Number Three oarsman.

Ben stared miserably at the eight exhausted men in front of him.

Other boats skimmed by. The wash tossed their boat chaotically, sending water slopping over the sides.

Ben's trainers were soaked and the life-jacket he was wearing for padding had risen up high on to his shoulders making him feel like an American footballer and exposing the very part of his body which needed most protection.

As the boat jerked forward at each pull of the crew's blades, the piece of wood which jutted out behind him seemed to gouge out lumps of skin from the small of his back.

And now they had all started shouting at him again.

When they had done it earlier Ben had put it down to nerves from having had to wait so long at the beginning of the race. Because there were over three hundred boats entering the Head it had to be staggered. They were number 183. Sitting huddled together hemmed in by the other boats they had grown stiffer and tenser by the minute.

They'd had a jerky start but no jerkier than anyone else so that Ben had been totally unprepared for the sudden onslaught of venom from his crew. Screaming, 'Over to the right, you blithering idiot!' at him and, 'No, you cretin, to the left!' Ben had gaped at them, stunned, as they had shot towards him on their seats, hollering.

Even when they slid away from him pulling their blades through the water there was no relief. They still glared at him and within seconds they were all shooting forward in his direction again and he would find himself almost nose to nose with Stroke.

And then there was the pain.

With each accelerated jerk the small of his back was repeatedly hit. It was all he could do not to cry out. Instead he blushed furiously as the eight yelling men continued to propel themselves towards him and away again.

Was this the pleasant-tempered team he had trained with on those balmy evenings on the river? he had asked himself. But then on their training sessions they hadn't taken much notice of him. They had been too busy listening their coach as he rode along the bank on his bicycle issuing instructions through a loudspeaker. And there had been few boats to bother them. They had had mostly only herons for company. Eventually, to his relief, they had settled into a steady rhythm, leaving Ben to steer them among the flotilla of boats streaming jaggedly down the river.

He tried to relax, but his forehead ached from frowning away the sun which was bouncing off the water into his eyes. He pulled down the peak of his cap but it only meant he had to raise his chin to keep an eye on the crew.

He tried to change position in the tiny space, drawing his knees even closer to his chest. Huddled into a tight ball his legs felt so stiff he wondered if he'd ever walk again.

He gazed forward at the long slim boat which now seemed about a mile long. The broad-shouldered Number Four was baring his teeth at him. He was the tallest of the men and mega serious. He came in for weight and circuit training at least three or four times a week.

Stroke trained seriously too, but usually he enjoyed it. Now he too was staring at Ben grim-faced.

It was all right for them, thought Ben. He had to learn on his own. They could easily find people to coach them so they could improve their rowing. Finding someone to coach a cox was impossible.

He felt pent up with frustration. He wanted to help them but he wasn't sure what to tell them. He didn't even have his dad to help patch up his mistakes.

He mustn't panic, he told himself fiercely. He must keep reminding himself that he was in charge, but it felt strange at only thirteen to be telling a crew of thirty to forty-year-olds what to do. Some of them were even older than his father.

'Now what are you doing?' yelled the Number Four again. 'Move us over!'

Ben knew they couldn't move yet. They would have

had to cut a corner. Dad said he must never do that. Besides, he had a vague feeling they would be heading for dead water.

'Give us the orders, come on!' joined the Number Seven. 'Use your bloody eyes!!'

And then they all joined in, including Stroke.

Ben lost his nerve. He glanced quickly behind him. Perhaps they were right. After all, they were more experienced.

He started to give out orders to the individual oarsmen.

They slowed down. They were in dead water. His instinct had been right.

'Couldn't you see there's no current here?' yelled the Number Two.

'But you asked me . . .' he began.

'You're not supposed to obey us,' snapped Stroke. 'We're supposed to obey you. Now get us out of here.'

Two eights swept past them, their blades narrowly missing clashing against theirs.

'In. Out,' yelled Ben, his voice shaking with anger and hurt. 'In. Out.'

'Now where are you taking us?' screamed the Number Four.

'Only to the middle of the river,' panted the Number Seven. 'Take us to the fastest part.'

The middle is the fastest part, thought Ben. At least, that's what he thought. But then nobody seemed to know for sure. Everyone had their theories, which all conflicted with one another.

'Watch out,' yelled a cox from a nearby boat. Ben gave the individual orders to straighten out.

'Right,' he muttered. 'Since everything I do is a

mistake, I might as well make a big one. In. Out,' he yelled quickly. 'Come on! Keep together!'

'You're taking us too fast,' gasped Stroke.

'In. Out,' repeated Ben, ignoring him.

They were really moving now. Ben was right. The middle of the river was faster, and with the additional rowing speed they were moving at a tremendous pace.

'We'll never keep this up,' said the Number Two.

'Quiet in the boat,' yelled Ben. 'You're wasting energy.'

And then they hit a mooring buoy.

Ben didn't care. In the distance he could see the bend in the river. There were two eights behind him and one ahead. He had to get in between them otherwise they would be left behind and thrown back into dead water. He knew he had to time it so that their boat was near the edge when they went round the bend. He could see from what the other eights were doing that they all agreed that that was where the fastest bit of the river was.

He gave the orders to move.

They were moving too fast to avoid another buoy. It clunked against the side of the boat and rocked wildly.

He could hear furious yells coming from somewhere and he knew they were aimed at him.

'That's their water,' said Stroke, alarmed, referring to the boat behind them. 'If we move into that we'll be disqualified.'

Now he tells me, thought Ben.

Within seconds he steered to the starboard side.

'Oh my giddy aunt!' panted the quieter Number Three. 'Make up your mind will you?'

A crew of eight passed them. Out of the corner of his eye Ben saw them swerve too close to the bank. They careered into one of the moored houseboats knocking one of the blades out. As the blade went flying in the air, Ben could see the crew angrily waving their fists at their girl cox even though it wasn't her fault.

Ben felt for her. Being a cox was like being a human punch-bag.

'Watch out!' yelled an eight on their port side.

They didn't make it to the edge of the water.

His crew were furious. Ben could understand why. Working as hard as they could they had to endure seeing other crews not making so much effort but moving faster because they had been coxed into the fast current.

'In. Out,' yelled Ben, his voice growing hoarse.

'Now where are we going?' yelled out the Number Two.

Luckily, being a veteran team, their boat didn't rate having a cox box-loudspeaker. Otherwise his muttered, 'I haven't the faintest idea,' would have resounded all down the river.

By some fluke they found themselves back in good water and were picking up speed.

'In. Out,' he yelled. 'In. Out.'

They were racing along at a fantastic rate. It was wonderful. His spirits soared. At last he had done it. It had taken him nearly the whole race to get it together, but they hadn't been disqualified or capsized or lost a blade.

He grinned with the sheer exhilaration of it.

Until he saw the eight ahead.

It didn't take him long to work out that their crew were not rowing as fast as his. In fact they looked spent. What was he to do? His crew were rowing magnificently, their blades rising out of the water in perfect unison, turning and scooping the water in beautiful measured time.

If he made them slow down all their hard work would go for nothing. If he didn't, they would crash straight into the boat in front. He continued to urge them on. He knew he was being stupid, but he couldn't stop himself. He was hoping for a flash of inspiration or that somehow they would be able to fly.

Someone in the crew in front started to point wildly over their cox's shoulder. The cox glanced swiftly round with a look of horror.

Within seconds she was giving orders for her crew to move out of the way.

Ben watched his boat heading directly towards its stern. They were almost on top of them. As they passed them, their oars clashed.

'Keep calm,' yelled Ben. 'In. Out. In. Out!'

And then they were through and he heard the crew they had scorched past fall yelling into the water and he knew they had capsized.

He glanced at his team. To his amazement his Number Four and Number Seven were smiling. They were the only members of his team who were. The others looked as if they were wondering whether to put up their life insurance subscriptions or take up golf instead.

To his shame Ben still didn't care. He concentrated on getting his crew back into a steady rhythm. They had beaten another eight. It seemed daft to get so excited about it when there were so many boats in the Head Race. But he had coxed them into good water and kept them there.

The crew were beginning to flag, their vests sodden with sweat. The Number Five looked so red that if the top of his head had popped off, Ben wouldn't have been surprised to have seen steam erupting from it.

Ahead of them was a bridge. Beyond that it was a mere 100 metres to the club's pontoon.

'Keep together,' Ben yelled. 'Drive with your legs!'

He had heard one of the older coxes use that expression so he thought he'd chuck it in for good measure.

'We're nearly home,' he yelled.

'I'm not going to make it,' groaned the Number Five.

'Of course you're going to make it,' Ben screamed. 'You're rowing fantastically. Come on. Keep going. In. Out. In. Out.'

And they were back into a steady rhythm again, everyone pulling in unison.

It was at that moment that another eight appeared. They were a schoolboy team. At a glance Ben figured that the oldest couldn't be older than 15 or 16. To Ben's amazement he saw 302 emblazoned on the back of the cox. They must have started way after them and here they were gracefully gliding alongside them.

His Number Four and Number Seven jutted their jaws out in anger.

'Come on,' yelled Number Four. 'They're beating us! Get us in the right water.'

But Ben knew it wasn't because they weren't in good water. The schoolboy team was faster because they were better, fitter, and younger.

'Come on, keep going,' he yelled hoarsely. 'We can do it!'

'We're going as hard as we can,' panted out the Number Five angrily.

'In. Out. In. Out,' screamed Ben. 'Push your paddles away!'

But it was no use. The schoolboy team was past them

and everyone in his crew was calling Ben every four letter word Ben knew, and a few he didn't.

Ben was so panic-stricken that he didn't see through his eight burly crew a boat stopping in front of them. By sheer fluke they missed it, but only just.

'Are you going to bloody cox us or not?' yelled Number Four.

'Give me strength!' roared Number Seven.

'Look behind you,' yelled Stroke.

Ben took a quick look. Several eights were skimming towards them. In the time it took him to whirl round, Ben realized that they were boxed in at the side by even faster eights, sending them swaying to the starboard side of the river directly towards the bridge.

He couldn't order his crew to slow down. They'd be hit from behind. Visions of other people's flailing blades concussing his exhausted crew descended on him.

With horror he watched his crew speed towards the bridge.

'We're going to hit the bridge!' he yelled.

'Stop us then, you berk.'

How can I? thought Ben. We're hemmed in.

It was weird. He knew they were hurtling along, yet it seemed as if they had suddenly gone into slow motion.

He swallowed.

'Go easy,' he said weakly.

Should he get them to drop their blades into the water to slow them down? No, they'd still crash and some of the blades were bound to get broken. As he tried to think of a way out he suddenly realized that they were making no headway. He had lost steerage. The rudder was simply refusing to obey him. Helpless he watched the boat swing round like a piece of driftwood.

'Drop your blades!' he screeched.

The current was bringing them down nearer the bridge, broadside on.

'Fend off!'

They hit the bridge. The boat gave a huge jolt. The short stocky Number Six lost grip on his blade. The handle swung back wildly, hitting him hard under the chin and sending him sprawling backwards with such force that his head hit the Number Five squarely in the belly.

Already a deep red, the Number Five's face turned instantly purple. Ben stared horrified at him as he opened and shut his mouth, fighting for breath. It looked as though he was going to have a heart attack on his hands and he wouldn't even be able to get to him to give him the kiss of life.

The boat gave a sudden lurch. Stroke, now ashen, leaned towards Ben and vomited.

Ben clung to the sides of the boat as it rocked, the peak of his cap and his clothes dripping. And he came to a decision. He would not look down.

In an instant he realized that they still had a chance. The boat hadn't sunk and none of the blades had been broken. But most important of all, they were still moving. If they had stopped it would have taken his crew for ever to get their shocked muscles into gear again.

The pontoon was only 100 metres away. A hundred metres and it would all be over.

He grappled for something to say. He had heard one of the more experienced coxes in their club yell, 'Take me home,' when her crew had almost reached the end of a race.

What he hadn't realized was that it was the sort of

command you gave in a regatta to a crew who were lengths ahead of the only other crew. The command gave them a chance to relax and catch their breaths before their final winning spurt.

As Ben watched his crew floundering and attempting to push themselves away, he yelled with as much of a commanding voice as he could muster.

'Take me home!'

'Shut up, you little punk,' yelled the Number Two.

'Did he say "Take me home"?' screamed the Number Four. 'I'll take him home all right. I'll take him to the bloody cleaners.'

'We haven't got eyes in the backs of our heads,' said the Number Three. 'Give us some instructions!'

Ben gulped.

With so many boats streaming past them, they sat, their blades held clear of the water while the wash sent them rocking violently back to the wall of the bridge.

'If you don't get us moving,' rasped Stroke in his face, 'we'll stop altogether and we'll never get started again.'

Ben spotted the tiniest gap appearing between two boats.

'Paddle on One and Three. Pull,' he yelled, and he eased the rudder gently.

But his crew were falling apart. The sudden episode with the bridge after the frenzy of rowing had left them uncoordinated.

Ben crossed his fingers. 'Come on everyone. In. Out. In. Out.'

By a miracle they somehow managed to pull themselves into the gap. Sluggishly and laboriously they headed for the pontoon.

'Never again,' muttered Ben, sponging down the hull of the boat with wide angry strokes. 'Never, never again!'

Ever since he had started washing the boat down he had been trying to wipe out the memory of their arrival at the pontoon.

Having swallowed down his embarrassment he had had to go through the whole procedure of telling them to unscrew the blades and pick the boat up out of the water. While they had carried it coffin-like on their shoulders to the section of the field apportioned to their club's boats, the umpire had stopped them to tell him off for hitting two buoys and to disqualify them for causing a boat to capsize.

But it hadn't been that which had incensed his crew. Or the crash into the bridge. It was the fact that they had been beaten by a crew of schoolboys which had left them smarting.

Once the boat had been stacked they had surrounded Ben and towered over him haranguing him.

Even mild-mannered Stroke was fuming, though he did tell the Number Four to 'lighten up' when he had threatened to spit-roast Ben.

There wasn't even a chance for Ben to apologize, and anyway it seemed pointless. They wouldn't have been in the mood to accept it even if they had heard it.

As soon as they had abandoned him to take their showers, Ben began his usual task of cleaning down the boat. It was part of a cox's duties. A crew was always too exhausted to do it.

He threw the sponge into the bucket and rested his head on the boat for a moment, still trying to erase all the names he had been called.

A sudden hissing sound made him whirl round with fright.

Peering round a row of boats stacked in tiers behind him he saw a mop of tangled red hair. It was Mandy, one of the other coxes. She was a year older than him.

'You made me jump. What are you doing?' he asked.

'Hiding.'

'From your crew?'

'No. From Bill. He'll kill me when he finds out what I've done. There's a twelve-foot gash in our boat.'

'What happened?'

'We hit an island. What am I going to do?'

'I don't know. I know what I'll be doing though. I'll be back to rowing with my family. That's if they don't chuck me out of the Rowing Club.'

'Yes. I heard your lot. They were pretty foul, weren't they?'

Ben nodded. 'Dad warned me some of them might throw a wobbly, but I didn't really believe him. No wonder they find it difficult to get a cox. It's a mug's game. Look at this,' he said, presenting the front of his T-shirt. He turned round and hauled it up.

'And this!'

A huge dark bruise fanned out round the base of his spine.

'And I ache everywhere. And for what? A bellyful of flack.'

'At least you're alive,' she said encouragingly. 'And no one got drowned, did they?'

'No,' he said miserably. 'But my chances of coxing in a race again have been scuppered.'

'You mean you want to go through it again?' asked Mandy, amazed.

'Yes,' he said, surprised. 'I suppose I do.'

'You're as mad as I am.'

Suddenly, she looked over his shoulder and gave a yelp. Ben swung round. A Land Rover was approaching. The driver was in his 40s, tanned and with a thick moustache. It was Bill. He leaned out of the window, smiling with amusement at Mandy, who had taken off at a sprint.

'What's up with her?' he called out.

'She thinks you're going to kill her. Her boat's got a huge gash in it.'

To Ben's alarm Bill leapt out of the car and ran after her.

'Why didn't I keep my big mouth shut?' he muttered.

But in the distance he could hear Bill yelling, 'Hey! Mandy! I can patch that up. No problem. Come back!'

Ben glanced down at his clothes. He smelt terrible. There was no getting away from it. He would have to take a shower. With any luck his crew would have taken theirs by now.

But he picked up the chamois-leather and began rubbing the hull vigorously as another delaying tactic.

There must have been a long queue for the shower, for the first thing Ben heard as he entered the adjoining cloakroom was his crew's voices echoing under the running water.

He sank quickly on to a bench in the corner, hiding himself behind the track suits which had been flung over the hooks.

Gingerly he took off his sodden cap and dropped it on the floor.

He had showered masses of times with other men, so it wasn't out of embarrassment that he was avoiding taking off his clothes. He just wasn't used to showering with his own crew. Usually, after a training session, by the time he had hosed and rubbed down the boat, they were already in the bar having a welcome pint.

Suddenly, the thought of being naked with eight furious men made him feel extremely vulnerable.

A loud roar of laughter from the shower caused him to raise his head. Up till that moment he had managed to shut out the noise.

'And when your head went thwack into my gut,' he heard the Number Five say, 'I thought I'd be pushing up the daisies.'

'So did I,' said the Number Six, wryly.

'What about when he said "Take me home",' put in the Number Five. 'I'll never forget that.'

'Priceless,' added the posh Number Three, and they all fell about laughing again.

Ben was burning with embarrassment.

'I'll live off that for months,' said the Number Seven.

'And did you see the expression on that cox's face when we scraped past her? I couldn't stop smiling.'

Ben was stunned. They were already telling anecdotes about the race as if they had enjoyed it!

'Best Head Race I've been in for years,' said the Bow.

'Yes,' said Stroke. 'Let's hope no one tries to nab him. Any cox is difficult to get, but a good one . . .'

The others voiced their agreement.

Ben couldn't believe it. Was this the man who had snarled at him, called him the cretinous runt of an orang-utan, and vomited all over him?

It didn't take Ben long to twig that although their anger had been directed at him, they had really been angry with themselves.

They started to talk about the team who had hit the houseboat and then the Number Four and Number Seven started singing.

Ben could have sung out loud with them. They actually wanted him to cox for them again! Tears of relief blurred his vision. Hastily, he pressed his fingers hard into his eyes in case anyone walked in and saw him.

Once he had pulled himself together, he peeled off his clothes, flung his towel round his waist sarong style, took a deep breath and sauntered casually towards the showers.

LOST

Kathy drifted in and out of a fevered sleep. She wedged herself further into the back of the sofa and dragged the duvet up over her shoulders. Her face was burning but her body was so cold she could feel the goose-pimples stretching her skin.

Exhausted, she fell asleep, but her raw throat dragged her back into consciousness again. That and the wind which was rattling the sitting-room windows.

She curled herself round her hot-water bottle. It was lukewarm but she was too cold to go into the kitchen and refill it.

The phone started ringing. Kathy ignored it. Her mother said she wasn't to answer the phone or the door.

She should have been in bed, but her mother had allowed her to lie on the sofa and watch television as long as she promised to keep warm. If she found her playing the piano when she popped home in her lunch-hour, she would take the afternoon off work to keep an eye on her.

Kathy didn't want her to do that. Her mother had been much happier since she had stopped being on the dole and had started her job as a dental assistant. Not wanting her to lose her job, Kathy had neglected to mention that as well as a temperature, she also had a sore throat and a headache.

The telephone stopped ringing.

The wind was louder now. Earlier Kathy had tried to watch television but she had had to turn up the volume so often because of the howling outside that it had made her headache worse, so she had switched it off.

The phone gave two rings and then suddenly stopped.

Kathy pulled the duvet cover over her head in an effort to block out the wind's roar and sank back to sleep. But it entered her dreams. Through its whistling and moaning a disembodied voice was calling out to her.

She opened her eyes but she could still hear it.

'Kathy! Kathy!'

If she hadn't been feeling so ill she would have sworn it was her mother's aunt from up the road.

The calling persisted.

'This is crazy,' she croaked.

She hauled her aching limbs into a sitting position.

Bobbing in front of her eyes were her slippers and the cat's ball. One of her sister's bears glided by.

She closed her eyes hurriedly. What was happening to her? Perhaps she should ring her mother. She had promised her she would if she felt worse.

There was a loud hammering at the front door. She opened her eyes again, but everything still seemed to be swimming about. The hot-water bottle slipped off the sofa and gave a loud splash. To her horror she discovered that her duvet was trailing in a foot of brown sludgy water. The water had completely surrounded the sofa and was rising fast. Shocked, she realized that she was sitting on an island that would soon be submerged.

A loud crash made her swing round. The television had keeled over. It hit a nearby table sending a pile of freshly-ironed clothing toppling into the water. Kathy stared terrified as the flailing arms and legs of shirts and jeans stretched out only to be suddenly sucked below the surface.

She pushed herself back into the sofa. Numbed with panic she watched the water working itself up her duvet like oil soaking up the wick of a lamp.

It dawned on her then that if she waited to be rescued she might suffer the same fate as the clothing.

Cautiously she lowered her legs into the murky liquid. It rushed round her legs startling her with its iciness. Dizzy and hot, she swayed, her ears aching from her sore throat, and then she began to shake and rattle as uncontrollably as the glass in the windows.

Once standing she could see past the cat ornaments on the window-sill and out across the road to the other bungalows.

Water was swirling into the front doors. An elderly couple were being helped through their flooded front garden by a neighbour. The woman was crying.

'Kathy! Kathy!' repeated the voice in the wind.

'Aunt Joanie!' shouted Kathy frightened. 'Is that you?' But her mother's aunt only repeated her name.

'I'm coming, Aunt Joanie. I'm coming.'

She paddled gingerly towards the door, her mum's new carpet squelching under her feet.

Once in the passage she could hear Daisy miaowing piteously from her bedroom. She hesitated for a moment.

'Kathy! Are you all right?' shouted her great-aunt.

'I'm coming.'

Something hard hit her legs. She drew back sharply

but it was only the telephone. She struggled past floating boots and newspapers, gripped the latch of the door and pulled it open.

The gush of water which swept in nearly toppled her over. Her great-aunt grabbed her.

'Oh, Kathy,' she said, 'I'm that relieved. What kept you? Why didn't you answer the phone?'

Kathy stared blankly at her. From the knees up her aunt stood as small and as well turned out as usual in her pale beige raincoat with matching scarf and handbag, her grey hair neatly permed. But from the knees down there was nothing but brown water.

'What's happening?' asked Kathy, bewildered.

'The sea-wall's broken. You've to come over to my place before the water gets too high.'

'I'd better phone Mum.'

'The phones are out of order. She'll realize you're with me. I promised to keep an eye on you. Put your anorak and scarf on and we'll go.'

'I can't leave Daisy. She'll drown.'

'She won't. Cats are very agile.'

'Daisy isn't. She's too fat.'

Only last night her mother had told her off yet again for giving Daisy too many titbits. Kathy was sure she didn't give her that much, but her mother blamed her for Daisy's gain in weight.

'She must be getting the food from somewhere else,' Kathy protested as Daisy grew more pear-shaped by the day.

'All right,' said her great-aunt, seeing how anxious Kathy was, 'but hurry, the water's rising.'

Daisy was in Kathy's bedroom perched on her chest of drawers. Kathy edged her way towards her, her legs impeded by floating clothing which coiled around her like tentacles. From now on she'd be tidy. She'd never leave her books or clothes on the floor ever again.

Daisy stared at Kathy with her huge green eyes and watched her struggling through the debris. As soon as Kathy reached her she leapt on to the bedside table, knocking the lamp into the water.

'Come on, Daisy, I'm not going to hurt you. Please don't go Miss Independent on me now,' she pleaded.

She made a lunge towards her, but Daisy stumbled through her arms and fell screeching into the water. Kathy scooped her up and held her sodden body close to her chest.

'You're all right, my lovely Daisy,' she crooned. 'You'll be safe now, I promise.'

But Daisy protested loudly and dug her claws so hard into her that Kathy had to grit her teeth not to yell with the pain.

Still clutching the squirming cat she weaved in a stupor towards the sitting-room.

Standing in two feet of water was her beloved piano. She had only had it a few months. Three of her aunts had clubbed together to buy it for her. Even though it was second-hand it had cost a fortune.

Her mother had been furious at the time. There was no way she could have afforded piano lessons for Kathy but one of the teachers at Kathy's new school had encouraged her and had even been giving her extra lessons after school.

Her sister Tina said it was big and ugly, but all Kathy cared about was the sound it made. Even now she was tempted to play it.

Perched on the music-stand was her first composition. The tune had been easy, but setting it down on paper for the three instruments had taken her months of sweat.

She had called the piece 'Maelstrom' which she knew was a Swedish word for storm.

She glanced swiftly round for somewhere she could put it and lifted the lid of the piano-stool.

The music inside was already sodden.

'Kathy! What's keeping you?' her great-aunt cried.

Kathy thought quickly. She couldn't carry the score with Daisy in her arms. She was so wet the ink would run and she might drop it or the wind might blow it out of her hands. But she had to save it somehow. It was irreplaceable.

It was just as she was closing the lid of the stool that she remembered the lid of the piano. Daisy started to struggle again, miaowing vehemently. Kathy hung on to her.

'Stay still,' she commanded.

Struggling, she manoeuvred the angry cat under one arm, threw the lid back and thrust her composition inside.

'Coming,' she called out to Aunt Joanie.

A policeman stood outside her great-aunt's bungalow. They were too late. Water was already lapping against her front door knob.

'Sorry, love,' he said. 'You can't go in. We've to evacuate the area.'

'But my children,' Aunt Joanie protested.

The policeman looked alarmed.

'Children?' he began.

'They're ornaments,' explained Kathy quickly.

'Oh I see,' said the policeman. 'Sorry, madam, the water's rising fast.'

Kathy watched her great-aunt nod silently. It had taken years for her to collect her ornaments of children.

Many of them were souvenirs from holidays or bargains she had bought in local auctions and jumble sales.

'I'll organize a lift for you to a rest centre.'

'That's all right,' said Aunt Joanie. 'I have a niece who lives in a house higher up.'

'Are you sure she'll be home?'

'Yes. She works from there.'

'You all right, love?' asked the policeman, taking in Kathy's flushed face.

Kathy was shivering so uncontrollably she couldn't speak. Like her great-aunt, she nodded silently.

A woman on a lilo with a paddle passed by them. She was laughing.

'Coming in for a swim?' she called out to Kathy.

Kathy shook her head.

'She's got flu,' explained her aunt.

'Oh dear,' said the woman cheerfully.

'I don't know what she's got to smile about,' said Aunt Joanie. 'She must be a bit funny in the head.'

The woman must have heard her.

'I can't do any housework, can I?' she called back over her shoulder. 'I probably won't have to do any for days. Yippee!'

'There'll be tears before bedtime,' muttered Aunt Joanie, who always grew anxious if anyone was having too good a time. She glanced at Kathy.

'We must get some dry clothes on you. You'll catch pneumonia.'

Kathy went through her nodding routine again.

A fire-engine slowed down to give them a lift. It caused a huge wave to cascade over them so that even Aunt Joanie was soaked from her head down.

'Sorry,' said the driver, 'there's nothing I can do about it.'

Two of the firemen on board helped Kathy's great-aunt up to the front seat. Kathy was about to join her when she caught her foot on something hard. As she went flying Daisy gave a yowl and leapt from her arms.

In an instant Daisy was perched, fur raised, on a floating chair which smashed into a gate. She leapt on to a wall.

Kathy tried to run after her, but the two firemen held her back. 'Daisy,' she yelled. 'Daisy. Come back.'

She fought with the firemen but they were too strong for her. Once next to her aunt in the cab of the engine she broke down and cried. She was still crying when Auntie Phil opened her front door.

Auntie Phil was one of her mother's sisters and the oddball of the family. She always wore huge colourful ear-rings which were either fish or exotic birds. She even had a necklace with parrots hanging from it.

She dragged them in, delighted and relieved to see them. Usually Kathy was pleased to visit her but now nothing could console her for losing Daisy.

'I've laid some clothes out for you on the bed, Aunt Joanie. They should fit you.'

While Aunt Joanie went upstairs to change, Auntie Phil peeled off Kathy's sodden pyjamas and rubbed her down. Kathy just stared at her blankly while her arms and legs were pushed into dry clothes.

She looked down at the trousers her aunt had put on her. They had an orange, black and turquoise design on them. The sweater was bright turquoise and the shirt underneath orange. Her aunt was making an extra hole in the belt so that Kathy could keep the trousers up, which were now folded over about ten times.

She threw some thick woollen socks at her.

'These will help keep the wellies on.'

The wellies were massive but at least they were black and not turquoise with orange spots!

'You don't mean I'll have to go out dressed like this,' said Kathy horrified.

'I go out like it,' said Auntie Phil.

Yes, thought Kathy, but you don't mind.

Tears started rolling down her face again.

'I want to talk to Mum,' she sobbed.

'The telephone lines are down,' her aunt reminded her.

'What about Tina?' she wailed. 'She's so tiny she'll be drowned.'

'Her teachers will make sure she's safe, don't you worry.'

'But I *am* worried, Auntie Phil. And there's Daisy. I've lost Daisy.'

Auntie Phil drew her close.

'And I had to leave the piano!'

It was the last straw.

Auntie Phil held her tightly until Kathy cried all the tears out of herself. It was while she was blowing her nose that they noticed Aunt Joanie.

Aunt Joanie never wore trousers. Kathy had never seen her in anything else but a pale skirt with a matching jersey and cardigan.

She now stood in the kitchen doorway drowned in a red and yellow track suit with a huge cockatoo on the front. Her perm had gone so berserk that it looked as though someone had plugged her into an electric socket with the power full on.

Kathy took one amazed look at her and began to laugh so hysterically that she had hiccups.

'Philippa, I can't be seen like this,' began Aunt Joanie.

But Auntie Phil was rolling around the kitchen completely helpless.

'You'd look nice,' she shrieked, 'if it wasn't for your hair.' And she leaned against the kitchen cabinet gasping.

Aunt Joanie's lower lip trembled.

'It's all right for you,' she began shakily, 'you haven't had to leave your home and all the things you've collected and worked hard to buy. It's cruel of you. Cruel. And in front of Kathy.'

And to their astonishment she burst into tears.

'I don't need the flood to reach here,' said Auntie Phil later when they had all recovered and eaten their way through a mound of sandwiches in the sitting-room. 'There's been enough tears in my kitchen to float us all.'

Kathy gave Aunt Joanie a smile, but her great-aunt was staring into space looking pale and lost amongst the clutter of newly-knitted jumpers and dwarfed by Auntie Phil's knitting-machine.

Kathy turned hurriedly away and sipped her mug of lemon and honey.

'Auntie Phil, I'm really worried about Mum and Tina.'

'I know, love. And I bet she's worried about you. But we just have to be patient.'

Aunt Joanie started making gasping noises. They whirled round to look at her. She was pointing wildly at the floor.

'What is it, Aunt Joanie?' asked Auntie Phil. 'Are you feeling ill?'

But her great-aunt couldn't answer. Instead she just waved her outstretched hand at the carpet, her mouth silently opening and shutting.

They looked down.

Soundlessly, brown liquid had oozed under the door and was making its way across the floor to a pile of red and blue wool.

*

Five days later Kathy, Tina and her mother stood outside their bungalow for the first time since the twenty-foot-high waves had sliced through the sea-wall.

For five days they had stayed with another aunt who lived on the hill. Although there was no risk of flood water reaching them Aunt Joanie still kept her eyes rivetted to the floor and had grown so frightened of water that she refused even to get into a bath.

It hadn't been till nearly 11 o'clock on the day of the flood that Kathy's mother had arrived with Tina at her Auntie Bethan and Uncle John's. And then there were hugs all round and exchanges of flood stories.

There were now ten people living in her Auntie and Uncle's house. Kathy shared a bedroom with Tina and her mother. It was cramped, but they knew they were lucky. Other people had had to queue for rooms at hotels or stay in an old castle which had been opened up to flood victims.

'We'd better face the music,' commented Kathy's mother, glancing at their open front door.

'Or see if it's still there,' muttered Kathy, thinking of her composition.

As they squelched through the dead grass, a foul smell erupted from the ground.

'Ugh!' said Tina, holding her nose. 'It stinks.'

The curtains were still hanging in the sitting-room window as though nothing had happened, so it was a shock when they entered the front passage.

It was as if they had never lived there. The flood had swept all trace of Tina, Kathy and her mother out the door. The entire floor area was mud. A quick glance and they saw how high the water had risen on the mottled damp walls. Higher than Kathy.

'Thank goodness you woke up,' said her mother quietly.

They took a few steps in. Sticking up through the mud and rotting rugs were floor-boards. The stench was terrible.

'It's a mess,' said Tina.

Kathy raised her eyes. Her sister always had a habit of stating the obvious.

Standing there with bin-bags and cleaning materials, a J-cloth seemed about the daftest thing to be carrying.

'What we need is a shovel,' commented their mother.

They forced their way through the sludge in the passage, carefully avoiding the gaps in the floor-boards.

'Yeuk!' said Tina pointing with disgust down one hole. 'Worms!'

'Oh, Kathy,' her mother whispered, 'I'm so sorry, but I'm afraid your piano will be ruined.'

'Good,' said Tina cheerfully. 'I won't have to listen to you practising any more.'

'And I won't have to listen to you practise your disco dancing,' added Kathy.

'What do you mean?'

'Your cassettes will be lost too,' explained her mother.

'Well we can buy some more,' she said matter-of-factly.

'Tina, I'm afraid cassettes will be at the bottom of my list for necessary things to buy.'

Tina's face fell.

'We won't be going to auctions again for furniture, will we?'

'I'm afraid so, love.' She turned to Kathy. 'You'll have to wait a while for another piano too.'

'I know,' said Kathy.

They stood in the mud while their mother poured them cups of tea from a thermos.

'We'll have to have new floors first,' said their mother quietly. She sighed. 'There's a lot to be done before we can even think of furniture. Rewiring, replastering, re-decorating, re-everything else.'

'Where will we get the money from, Mum?' asked Kathy.

'Insurance, I hope. Thank goodness your Aunts gave you that piano.'

'I don't understand . . .' began Kathy puzzled. 'What's that got to do with money?'

'Because they gave it to you, I was forced to take out insurance for the contents of the house. That's why I was so angry about it. I couldn't afford it. Thank goodness I paid up!'

'We could go back to living in a caravan,' suggested Tina.

'I saw a caravan floating on its side in the flood,' said Kathy quietly. 'A house is safer.'

'Aren't we going to do anything today then?' asked Tina.

'I don't think we can,' said her mother. 'Not on our own. I suppose I'd better let your aunts help me after all.'

'Dad could come and help,' said Tina eagerly.

'You know he can't leave Sonia. Her baby's due any day now.'

Tina scowled. 'You shouldn't have left him. Then he wouldn't be with her.'

'I didn't,' said her mother wearily.

'Well you shouldn't have left London. We wouldn't have got flooded then.'

'I couldn't have afforded a place in London,' she pointed out. 'And anyway, if we hadn't come here, you wouldn't have got to know all your aunts.'

'But there are so many of them,' she grumbled. 'And they're always going on about Kathy.'

'Don't be silly.'

'Daisy's the only one who likes me and she's not here,' she said, glaring meaningfully at her sister.

Kathy looked guiltily away.

Her mother gave Kathy's shoulders a squeeze.

'You did your best.'

'One of the girls in my class put her hamster cage up high so that the water wouldn't reach her. You should have done that.'

'Daisy wouldn't have stayed there,' her mother argued.

'She would have if Kathy had put her in the cat basket.'

'There wasn't time,' explained Kathy.

'Of course there wasn't,' said her mother. 'And the cat basket could easily have fallen over and Daisy would have been drowned.'

'Well she has been anyway,' said Tina sulkily.

Kathy began to feel the tears welling up again.

'Tina, you weren't here. You don't know what it was like.'

'I had to be carried by one of the teachers, and then by a fireman. It was really good!'

'We know,' chorused Kathy and her mother, who had heard about Tina's experience so many times, they knew it by heart.

But Kathy agreed with Tina. She blamed herself for Daisy's loss. Her absence was the worst thing about their devastated bungalow. At her aunt and uncle's she had lain awake at nights worrying but still hoping. Now they had returned to find there was no sign of her she knew she hadn't survived. If she had made it back she would have been purring all over them or spitting at them for leaving her for so long, or miaowing for a feed.

The silence was like a great hole in her heart.

'What's that?' said her mother.

'Sounds like a bird,' said Tina.

From one of the rooms there was a faint high crying sound.

'A baby bird?' suggested Kathy.

They moved slowly up the passage trying to locate where the sound was coming from.

Hanging on to each other's arms they lifted their legs high and clambered over boxes and bits of piping, their boots weighed down by the mud.

'I think it's coming from the kitchen,' said Tina.

'What kitchen?' said her mother staring at the smashed cabinets hanging lopsidedly from stripped mildewy walls.

'A frog!' yelled Tina.

Tipped over on one side of a plank of wood was a stone frog. Tina leaned over, stretched out her arms and grabbed it. 'I've always wanted one of those!'

'That belongs to Mrs Wilson, Tina,' said her mother.

'But she hasn't got a garden to put it in any more,' said Tina.

'It's still Mrs Wilson's.'

'I'll look after it for her,' said Tina, struggling with it in her arms.

'That noise, it's coming from the sitting-room,' said Kathy.

'You're the one with the good ear,' said her mother. 'The sitting-room it is.'

'I have good ears too,' said Tina indignantly.

'And a good mouth,' added her sister.

'Thank you,' said Tina.

'That wasn't supposed to be a compliment,' said Kathy.

'Come on, you two,' said their mother. 'No time for squabbling. Kathy, I think you're right.'

'Oh, Mum,' wailed the girls when they entered the wrecked muddy sitting-room.

'I can't see us ever coming back,' muttered Kathy.

'We will. We've been through bad times before. And we've survived.'

'Shhh,' said Kathy. 'There it is again. It *is* in here.'

They stood listening while the wind shook the windows.

'Shhh wind,' ordered Tina.

'Oh, Mum,' whispered Kathy, 'look at the piano.'

Mottled and buckled it stood in a mound of mud and shingle.

'The lid's open,' commented their mother.

'I stuck my composition down there,' said Kathy. 'I must have forgotten to close it.'

'Pity you didn't think to put our photo albums in there too,' said their mother sadly.

'I'm sorry, Mum, there wasn't time.'

'It's all right, I know.'

It was then that they realized that the faint high-pitched noises were coming from the piano. Kathy and her mother struggled towards it and peered inside.

'You were right about the baby part of it,' whispered her mother, 'but not about the bird.'

Inside, bedded down on Kathy's score paper were two new-born kittens, their tiny umbilical cords still trailing from their stomachs across their damp fur. One of them had wrapped itself around the other.

'He's the strongest,' said Kathy's mother. 'Look, he's trying to keep that little one warm.'

'What is it? What is it?' said Tina impatiently.

'Kittens,' answered her mother. 'Two of them.'

'But how did they get there?' asked Tina.

'I think I know,' said her mother. 'And if I'm right, I owe you an apology, Kathy.'

'You mean Daisy wasn't fat, she was pregnant?'

'Yes. These must be two of the litter. She's probably dropped some others off on the way here.'

'But where is she?' demanded Tina.

'And why isn't she here?' added Kathy.

'I don't know.'

A plank overturning made them swivel round. Standing on a piece of rock stood Daisy, thinner and bedraggled, with a bird in her mouth.

'Ugh!' cried Tina.

'She's got to feed herself somehow,' said her mother, 'to keep up her milk supply.'

'Do you think she'll still like cat-food?' asked Kathy, 'or will she have gone wild?'

'I doubt it. Let's try.'

'I'm not going to cuddle her with that bird in her mouth,' pronounced Tina.

Kathy and her mother filled one bowl with cat-food and the other with water and put them down on the plank near her. They watched as she lapped from the two bowls with gusto and then started cleaning herself up.

'Ah,' said Kathy's mother. 'That's a good sign.'

After letting Kathy's mother give her a brief cuddle, Daisy leapt into the piano. The kittens buried their mouths into her fur and started sucking, their eyes closed.

'That brings back memories,' said Kathy's mother.

'What does?' asked Tina.

'Watching these kittens having their milk. It reminds me of feeding you two.'

'They look so comfortable,' commented Kathy. 'I think we ought to leave them there, don't you?'

'Yes,' agreed her mother. 'Lucky things. They must be the only two in the bay who aren't homeless.'

'We can bring food in for Daisy every day.'

'She'll look after the place,' said Tina.

'Yes, I think she will.'

'And you aren't cross she's had kittens?' asked Kathy.

'No. Before I saw them this bungalow didn't seem like our home any more. But as long as Daisy's here with them . . .'

'On my composition,' added Kathy.

Her mother laughed. 'Yes. We won't feel we've lost it.'

'I wish we could find one of Aunt Joanie's children,' said Tina, 'then she might feel the same. Eh, Mum?'

Kathy and her mother glanced quickly at one another.

Poor Aunt Joanie had gone to pieces. Her home was everything to her. She was always so particular, dusting and polishing her ornaments, changing her curtains fortnightly, and arranging the flowers from her garden in beautiful glass vases. Now all her possessions were either lost or submerged in mud. If anyone spoke to her, her face would crumple and the tears would spill from her eyes. Every time she cried, Auntie Phil would wrap her arms tightly around Aunt Joanie's tiny frame until she recovered.

'Perhaps she'd like one of the kittens,' suggested Tina.

'Now no pushing her,' said her mother. 'She's upset enough as it is.'

'When do you think she'll stop crying, Mum?'

'When she's ready.'

'Do you think it will be safe to live here again?' asked Kathy. 'The sea might come through the wall again. It might happen in the night when we're all asleep.'

'We won't come back until it's properly mended.'

Tina gave an impatient sigh. 'I'm bored,' she said. 'Let's go back to Auntie Bethan and Uncle John's. It's warmer.'

'And they've got a television,' Kathy added pointedly.

'I know just the place for this frog,' said Tina ignoring her. 'I'll put it in Auntie Bethan's bathroom. Until Mrs Wilson wants it back,' she added hurriedly. 'I bet she'll be pleased I've rescued it. I know what it's like to be rescued. I was carried by a teacher.'

'And a fireman,' chorused Kathy and her mother.

'Well I was!' exclaimed Tina.

Kathy, who had been resting her hand on the top of the piano, felt a rough tongue licking her fingers. It was Daisy. She had obviously been forgiven. While her sister and mother struggled through the mud and out of the sitting-room into the passage Kathy gazed down at the crumpled lined paper under the kittens.

'Percussion,' she whispered, feeling the old adrenalin suddenly returning, 'that's what I need.'

A great cacophony of sound like the sea crashing through the wall, she thought, and then maybe a solo flute piece after it. Flute? She'd never thought of trying to write music for a flute before.

She gave Daisy a hug. Thinking about her composition made her feel rooted again.

'We'll be fine now,' she whispered.

She glanced at the kittens. The larger tabby one had wrapped itself round the smaller black and white one again. Like Auntie Phil and Aunt Joanie she thought.

'We're going to miss my programme if she doesn't hurry,' she heard Tina saying insistently.

That was typical of Tina. As long as she could watch telly she felt at home anywhere.

'Kathy!' her mother called.

She gave Daisy a quick nuzzle and put her back down with her kittens.

'Coming,' she yelled.

As she waded back through the slime she noticed that the heavy feeling which had been dragging her spirits down for days had suddenly lifted and she didn't feel so frightened. She turned round for a last look at the piano.

Daisy was peering over it. She gave a loud miaow. Kathy smiled.

'Bye Daisy. See you tomorrow.'

SEA-LEGS

I

Tessa was flung violently against the side of the deep cockpit. Blinded by her fringe, she clung fiercely to the coaming with one hand and dragged her long brown hair from her eyes and mouth with the other. She had just managed to shove a tangled clump of it into her shirt, when a wave swept over the deck and broke against the doghouse. Before she could duck, a deluge of cold foam tumbled into the cockpit and streamed down the steps into the cabin.

She slid down and crouched, her face dripping, her baggy cotton sweater and trousers billowing damply around her. She had never expected the sea to be this rough, this cold or this terrifying.

She dragged herself up to the left side of the cockpit and thought wryly of the contents of her holdall, now thrown across the cabin. Inside it were textbooks and her swim-suit. She had planned to spend some time sunbathing before going below to do her homework. She had even imagined herself on deck waving to people in their colourful yachts as they glided alongside them in the sunlight. What a joke!

Suddenly the sodden mainsail above her head started to flap wildly and the next thing she knew she was being pushed firmly but gently aside. It was Joseph. He had sprung upwards towards her after casting off one rope and was frantically hauling in another. They were changing tack.

Tessa pinned herself against the back of the cockpit and stared up mesmerized.

'Boom coming over!' yelled Joseph to his friend at the helm. Like a fool, Tessa, who was miles out of reach, dropped quickly on to her heels as a thick piece of timber the size of a telegraph-pole arced over them. The boat lurched and she crashed to the floor hitting an elbow. By the time she had clawed herself up the boat was tipped so far on the other side that the sails were being pulled through the water.

Acutely aware that she was wearing no life-jacket or harness, Tessa wondered whether she would ever see her parents again. I want this to be over, she prayed, and soon.

It had seemed years since she had left Rye with her Uncle Nick and his two bachelor friends in the yacht. 'Yacht' was what her uncle had called it when chatting enthusiastically to anyone he could strike up a conversation about it with.

When he had taken her down to the moorings after lunch, she was stunned to find that it bore no resemblance to the glossy blue and white vessel she had imagined. Instead it was a 60-year-old wooden cutter, with peeling paint around her white hull.

Below decks inside the cabin, four old bunks were held up by chains. Standing solidly between them, to the front of the cabin, was the lower section of the huge wooden mast. As she stepped down she spotted a tatty two-burner stove on her left. Above the working surface beside it, plates were held in place by wooden batons near a row of stained mugs on hooks. To her right was a large dark varnished box, which she later discovered housed the engine. A chart was laid out on it.

She quickly realized that the chart table would be the only place she could do any of her weekend homework. There was no other furniture; no curtains by the three oval portholes on either side of the top bunks, and no carpets.

Tossed on to the wooden floor were ropes tied up in long loops and from the beams across the roof hung a couple of blackened oil-lamps.

Staring into the tacky gloom she had been speechless with disappointment. At least she could console herself with the thought that she wouldn't be spending the night in it. She could look forward to staying up late and getting spoiled by her uncle when they returned to his house.

The second surprise of the day was discovering that the cutter was owned by three men. Her family had always been given the impression that her uncle owned it outright and took a crew with him. The other two owners were friends, Joseph and Ted.

Joseph was hauling up the mainsail when they arrived, and Ted was twiddling a knob on a small transistor which was perched on a shelf under the doghouse.

She could tell by their faces they were surprised to see her.

Her uncle had hardly begun to talk nautical gobbledegook to her about jibs and staysails when Ted whirled round and snapped out, 'Shut up!'

To her amazement her uncle obeyed.

'Why should he?' she muttered crossly.

'Quiet!' he yelled.

'Is that how your crew speak to you?' she exclaimed.

'Shhh!' added Joseph, who was now leaning over the doghouse listening intently.

It was only then that she realized they were trying to listen to the weather forecast and had missed the essential bit because she and her uncle had been talking at the crucial moment. It didn't make for a great introduction.

Embarrassed, Tessa had sat hunched on the deck with her legs dangling into the cockpit. Luckily her uncle's friends were too busy preparing to sail to take much notice of her, so she took advantage of her invisible state to give them the once over.

Joseph was slim and wiry and always on the move, hauling or tying up ropes (though she discovered fairly quickly that the ropes attached to the sails were referred to as sheets). He sprang rather than walked, and when he spoke, it was excitedly and at a rapid rate. His blond hair and beard were bleached and tangled from sun and salt spray and his face was such a brick-red colour that his crooked teeth showed up white against his sunburnt mouth.

Ted was tanned too, but brown. He was quiet with dark hair and vibrant green eyes. Tessa had the impression that he didn't suffer fools gladly. She suspected he didn't like children either. When her uncle asked if anyone minded him bringing along his twelve-year-old niece, she had heard Ted mutter, 'It's a bit late to ask us if we mind now,' and later, 'This is not a crèche!'

Her uncle called out to her. He was untying the old car tyres they used as fenders. He handed them to her to chuck down on to the cabin floor.

'We have to move fast,' he explained. 'We only have an hour around high tide to get over the harbour bar and out into the sea.'

She had smiled up at him. He looked so nautical with

his salt and pepper beard, his navy cap, stripy T-shirt and white trousers. At least he was dressed for sailing, not like Joseph and Ted. They were actually wearing jumpers even though the sun was beating down on them. She had assumed it was because, being middle-aged, they felt the cold more.

Later she was to envy them those jumpers.

But then, sitting beside her uncle in the front, motoring happily down the river, protected by the mud-flats, their sails set ready for the open sea, she had felt as though she was about to embark on a great adventure. Warmed by the sun, accompanied only by the sounds of the chugging of the engine down below and sea-gulls, she brushed aside the awfulness of the boat itself and returned to thinking about her homework. As long as she could get at least half of it done it would be a successful afternoon. How could she have foreseen that as soon as the boat hit the open sea her uncle would be struck down by a mysterious illness and disappear into one of the bottom bunks where he would lie motionless, only to lift his head occasionally to commune with a large black bucket beside him; that she would be left alone with two men she didn't know – one of whom would have preferred her to have remained on shore – in a creaky old boat in gale-force winds. And if that wasn't enough, within half an hour of leaving Rye, she had been bursting for a pee but had been too embarrassed to ask for the loo. She knew there was one on board somewhere. Her uncle had mentioned it to her vaguely, only he had called it the 'Heads'.

She turned to speak to Joseph, but was shocked to discover he had gone. Terrified, she forced herself to cross over to the other side of the cockpit. Ted was perched high on the back of it hanging on to the tiller and staring sullenly out to the sea. Avoiding him she made a leap for the coaming, missed, and slid backwards on her hands and knees. She struggled to her feet and was about to fall again when he caught her by the collar, pulled her towards him and flung her on to one of the wooden steps below him.

'Thanks,' she gasped.

'What are you trying to do?' he yelled.

'See Joseph. Where is he?'

'On deck. Reefing,' answered Ted curtly.

The wind whistled and roared into her aching ears.

'Weeping?' she said, alarmed.

'Reefing,' he snapped. 'It means he's going to take in the sails a bit. Make them smaller, so that there's less power in them and we have more control of the boat.'

When he looked up sharply at the small flag at the top of the mast she gathered he didn't wish to speak any further.

She climbed up on to the step, pinned her arms over the coaming and peered out.

One of the front sails had been taken down, the staysail. The mainsail had been dropped half-way down the mast. Joseph was pulling it towards him in armfuls, rolling it and lacing it down to the boom. Each time the boat pitched, Tessa had to shove her knuckles into her mouth to prevent herself from screaming, for it looked as if he were about to be flung over the little rail that surrounded the boat and out into the sea. As he edged himself further along the boom and nearer the cockpit she willed him to survive. Joseph was her only hope. There was no way she could ask Ted where the toilets were.

As soon as he had thrown himself into the cockpit she felt safer. She took a deep breath but before she could open her mouth, he and Ted began a discussion about beating against a south-westerly wind.

'We'll just have to keep heading for Newhaven,' she heard Joseph yelling up to Ted.

'In this?' he cried. 'It could take till tomorrow.'

'Tomorrow!' shrieked Tessa, but her voice was smothered by the wind.

'There's no point returning,' shouted Joseph. 'We'd have to sail up and down this bay for about 12 hours waiting for high tide again. If we head for Newhaven at least we'll be going somewhere.'

Ted gave a nod and Joseph leapt down the steps in to the cabin. Tessa made a wild dash to the doorway and stumbled in after him.

'Joseph!' she yelled.

He was examining a chart on the lid of the engine-box. She touched his shoulder. He turned and smiled.

'Are we really not going back to Rye?' she asked anxiously.

'No. It would be too ignominious.'

'What does that mean?'

'Embarrassing. And it'd be too dangerous. The entrance to Rye is pretty choppy in bad weather. You should see how steep the waves get. Bigger boats than ours, even ones with powerful engines, have been wrecked there.'

He returned to the chart.

'Joseph,' she began. 'I was wondering . . .'

'What I'm doing?' he asked.

'Sort of. But first . . .' She hesitated.

It was in that moment of hesitation that they heard a loud rattling sound, like an underground train roaring underneath them.

'Good God!' cried Joseph, pushing her aside. 'What on earth's that?'

Tessa stayed on the top step and clung to the doorway paralysed with terror. She remembered having heard of submarines wrecking fishing boats. Any minute she expected the boat to be shattered into pieces underneath them. The two men, their faces alert, were scrutinizing everything in sight.

Suddenly Joseph gave a violent start.

'It's the chain,' he screamed, and he leapt out of sight.

Ted peered out towards the front of the boat alarmed, while the monstrous rattling sound continued to thunder beneath them. Imagining what was going on was too terrifying for Tessa. She threw herself against the coaming and craned her neck over it to see what was happening. It was then that she saw what was making the noise. Rattling at breakneck speed over the side of the boat was a large iron chain. Joseph was trying to stop it, but it was moving at such speed that it nearly took him with it. Tessa watched, riveted with fear, as he attempted to step on it with his foot, but it was useless. The chain continued to pour out.

'Ted, what's happening?'

She could see he was worried.

'The anchor's gone over the side.'

Joseph was sprinting along the deck towards them.

'If we don't stop the boat, the chain'll rip the deck out!' he hollered. 'Start the engine! Full astern! Put her head into the wind!'

'Take the tiller!' commanded Ted. 'And keep it steady.'

She jumped up on to the step, and grabbed it.

Ted was on his knees pulling at a small lever. The engine gave a low throttling sound.

The boat gave a lurch. Tessa gripped the tiller till she ached. It seemed that it was all that was between her and a watery death.

The next thing she knew she was buried in heavy wet canvas. She struggled to keep her legs braced on the step.

'Get the bloody sail off me!' she heard Ted yelling.

'I'm pulling it off as fast as I can,' came Joseph's voice through the wind.

'Are we going to drown?' Tessa whimpered.

'Not if I can help it,' grunted Ted from somewhere. 'Just stay put.'

Stay put! Where else could she go?

The boat pitched violently again.

Soaked and shaking Tessa felt the heavy canvas being pulled across her.

She hooked one arm firmly over the helm and shoved up a wedge of the sail with her free arm. But it was still too heavy for her to budge.

'Stop the engine!' she heard Joseph roar. 'It's useless in this sea. We're just turning in circles round the anchor.'

The engine spluttered to a halt.

'What's happened?' shouted Ted.

'We're in luck. The deck's intact. The bitter end hasn't come out.'

She heard Ted give a cry of relief.

Just then there was a clattering noise from below.

'Ted!' a voice called out.

It was her uncle.

'What?'

'Are we in Newhaven?'

Tessa heard a strangled, outraged snort.

'No!' Ted yelled. 'And we probably won't be there until tomorrow.'

There was a brief silence broken eventually by the muffled sounds of vomiting.

There was no need for him to be that harsh with her.

uncle, thought Tessa angrily. He was a sick man. How was he to know he would get food poisoning, or some virus, as soon as they left Rye?

She was about to come to his defence when she noticed that the canvas was no longer crushing her. She gave it a shove and managed to stick her head out. She gulped in the bitter wind, her hair rising up and round her head like a gorgon's. Joseph was hauling armfuls of mainsail up and shoving it round the boom. There was mainsail everywhere. It filled the cockpit, overflowed on to the deck and trailed into the sea.

From her high position she saw that the jib had been yanked down.

The canvas below her began to move. It was Ted fighting his way out. He pulled aside the sail and within seconds was heading towards the jib, clinging on to parts of the boat as he staggered towards the small trailing sail.

She watched him throw back a trapdoor, remove the jib, and sling it below. It was only then that she realized where the lavatory must be.

'So near, yet so far,' she murmured.

Ted joined Joseph and within minutes she felt the canvas being lifted from her shoulders.

The two men tied the remainder of the sail to the boom and half jumped, half fell into the cockpit talking rapidly in their nautical gibberish.

'I'll just have to sweat it up by hand,' Joseph was saying.

Ted clambered up on to the step and relieved Tessa of the tiller, not that it was doing anything. Tessa slid gratefully on to the step and leaned back.

Suddenly they stopped talking and she found that they were staring at her. She grinned up at them, her teeth chattering.

'Is that all the clothing you have?' inquired Joseph.

'Yes. But it's OK. I'm fine,' she said, shrugging it off bravely.

'I've a spare pair of socks, jeans and Guernsey on the bottom bunk,' he said. 'Put them on and grab some waterproofs and a hat from the pegs by the door behind the mast.'

'I'll be all right,' she said jovially, feeling like death.

'Don't be a martyr,' snapped Ted. 'We can't afford to have two sick people on board.'

'It's important to stay warm,' added Joseph gently. 'We don't want you getting hypothermia.'

'But only old ladies get that,' she protested.

'Don't you believe it. Anyone can get it out at sea.'

'OK,' she mumbled, and she reeled towards the cabin.

Suddenly she whirled round, 'Joseph,' she said puzzled. 'What's a Guernsey?'

2

Down in the dark cabin she glanced quickly at her sleeping uncle and back up to the cockpit. Ted and Joseph were still busy talking. Convinced that no one was watching, she hastily peeled off her sodden trousers and socks and pulled on Joseph's. She folded the waistband of his jeans over and made large turn-ups before lacing up her canvas shoes. The Guernsey was an old navy-blue jumper with stitching at the top of the sleeves just under the shoulders. She dragged off her soaked sweater and put it on. The warmth was immediate. With the cuffs rolled back she almost felt comfortable.

The boat gave another lurch flinging her against the mast. She hugged it and slid her way round to where the waterproofs were hanging. She had hardly let go when she was thrown against a door. Realizing it must be the door to the Heads, she turned the bronze handle. Nothing happened. In desperation she jammed her shoulder hard against it and gave a hefty push. It only budged slightly. And then she remembered the sails. They were obviously blocking the door. If she hadn't begun to feel queasy she could easily have howled with rage. She grabbed some yellow oilskins and an old tweed cap and scrambled back to the cockpit.

Feeling nauseous she hung her head over the coaming. The cold air buffeted and roared round her but it was heaven compared to the sick-making cabin. She began to hum rapidly. It was her cure for coach-sickness. She was praying it would have the same effect on a boat. As soon as the wind began to toss her hair about again she stuck the cap on and tucked any loose strands behind her ears. Still staring with fixed concentration at the sea she breathed in deeply and pulled on the oilskin jacket. Ted yelled at her.

She swung round alarmed.

'You put the trousers on underneath,' he explained. 'They'll cover your chest.'

Tessa could feel her face growing scarlet. As soon as she had spotted the braces she knew she had to put the trousers on first, but she wanted to wait until she had been to the Heads.

'I'll do it later,' she stammered, and turned hurriedly away to see what Joseph was doing.

He was sitting on the foredeck, his feet straddled

against the toe-rail, hauling up the heavy wet chain and tossing it into a heap behind him. With each convulsive heave of his body he gave a loud grunt. It was obvious he was using every ounce of his strength.

There was no way she could ask him to help her now. She hung vehemently to the coaming as the boat continued to be pitched about. Her stomach ached from controlling herself for so long, and every time the boat lurched, the pain made her feel sicker. She realized she would have to swallow her embarrassment and ask Ted.

When she looked up at him she found he was peering through a pair of binoculars. His expression was grim.

'Ted!' she yelled.

He glared down at her. 'How long do you think Joseph will be?' she asked nonchalantly.

He shrugged. 'There's sixty fathoms of chain. In these conditions it could take an hour. Could take three hours. Why?'

Against her will she heard herself saying, 'Just wondering when he'd like a cup of tea, that's all.'

For a fraction of a second she actually detected a slight smile.

'Later,' he said.

Miserable, she returned to staring at the sea.

'Idiot!' she muttered angrily to herself, and she pressed her forehead hard against her knuckles.

An hour later Joseph was still dragging up the chain on to the deck from his semi-crouched position. She watched him as he shoved each glistening pile of chain down a small hole in the deck before hauling the next lot up and looping it round the bitts on the fo'c's'lehead to prevent it sliding back into the sea.

As each section of chain was dropped down the hole, Tessa knew she was nearer salvation, but every time a length of it suddenly shot off the deck she would stop looking.

It was later that she noticed that Joseph was hauling up the chain with more ease. She called up to Ted.

'It's getting easier,' she shouted.

The frown on Ted's face visibly unfolded.

'That means we're above the anchor,' he hollered down to her. 'Only about another 80 feet of chain to go, at a guess.'

'How much is that in metres?'

He paused. 'About 25.'

She forced herself to smile, even though she was dying inside. But when she returned to peer over the coaming she was cheered to see relief on Joseph's face. Instead of having to put his back into it he was pulling in the chain, hand over hand.

'We've got it!' he yelled to them over his shoulder. 'Better get the main up, well reefed.'

Unable to take her eyes off the pile of chain which was heaped up on the deck and growing rapidly higher, Tessa could feel the excitement welling up inside her. When the anchor appeared over the side, a cry of sheer exhilaration erupted from her throat.

Ted leapt on deck.

Tessa climbed up on the back step nearest her and stopped the tiller from swinging. As she grabbed it she heard movement in the cabin. She glanced down quickly. Her uncle was by the galley, shakily pouring water from a big plastic container into a mug and swallowing some pills. Within seconds he had stumbled backwards out of sight and she turned to find Ted helping Joseph back into the cockpit.

Joseph collapsed on the floor, his legs spread-eagled, his back against the lockers. He looked as ashen as her uncle. She stared at him alarmed. 'Is everything all right?'

He nodded. 'Shackled down,' he gasped. 'It shouldn't give us any more trouble.'

Ted returned on deck and began hauling up the mainsail. Gradually the colour began to return to Joseph's face, but his arms and legs continued to shake uncontrollably. He caught sight of her staring at him and gave her a weak smile.

'Just tired,' he explained.

She nodded, attempting to smile back. What on earth was she going to do now? she thought. She couldn't ask him in this state.

'Frightened?' he asked croakily.

'A bit.'

'We'll survive.'

'Joseph,' she began, 'I need . . . would it be all right if . . .' She reddened.

'Do you want to go to the lavatory?'

She blushed and then to her amazement she added, 'But there's no hurry.'

Luckily he ignored her.

They made their way along the deck and Joseph went down into the Heads leaving Tessa on all fours gripping the edge of the open trapdoor. He gathered up an armful of the jib and pushed the remaining sail further against the cabin door to make more space around the lavatory seat.

The Heads was a small white painted cabin. Its wooden sides curved in towards a dark mahogany bench and beyond to a dark recess behind it where ropes and old life-jackets were stored. A porcelain lavatory bowl was in the centre of the bench and on one side of it were various levers.

'I'm opening the sea-cocks to let some water in,' Joseph explained. 'After you've been, pump this lever up and down. That'll empty it out into the sea. Don't forget to shut the sea-cocks off after you've finished, or you'll flood the boat.' He frowned. 'You're looking worried. Would you rather I did it? It's no trouble.'

'No thanks, I'll do it myself.'

He rummaged around under the staysail, dumped a roll of loo-paper on the top of it and hauled himself up through the hatchway dragging festoons of jib after him.

Tessa lowered herself in, stretching her legs out, but she was too small to reach anything. Joseph gripped her arms and dropped her into the staysail.

'Call when you're ready,' he said, peering down at her and he threw her oilskin trousers after her and closed the hatch.

With the wind shut off outside it felt quite snug in the secluded little cabin.

'Privacy,' she whispered.

Ten minutes later she was still sitting balanced on the sloping wooden seat staring at the brass lock on the small mahogany door in front of her. She had controlled her bladder for so long that her body had gone on strike. She buried her head in her hands, too numbed with cold and tiredness to cry.

The boat suddenly leaned to the other side. They must be changing tack. She braced her legs and looked around the cabin. It was surprisingly restful to be surrounded by creaking wood, with water gurgling beneath her in the bilges, or rushing past the hull outside. She glanced at the outboard motor lashed and bolted underneath the left porthole. The right porthole was under water.

Relieved at being able to drop the artificial smile she had fought to keep fixed since they had left Rye, she felt her face relax. It was at that moment that her body suddenly remembered how to work.

She flushed the lavatory, turned the sea-cocks off and dragged the oilskin trousers over her jeans, forcing the Guernsey down inside. The trousers came up to her armpits. She slipped the short braces over her shoulders, folded the bottoms up, and quickly put on the oilskin jacket.

Then she sat on the sail, the tweed cap in her hands, and stared out of the left porthole.

Mesmerized by the white foam bursting from green wave after green wave, she caught a glimpse of tiny houses in the distance perched high on vast rocky cliffs. The sky was tinged blood-red by the sun. She watched its fiery glow fall steadily until it disappeared behind the cliffs.

She leaned back into the folds of the staysail. She liked being in this little cabin. It was the only part of the entire nightmarish trip she had liked. Gradually, shadows began to lengthen across the white walls and she knew she would have to return to the cockpit before it grew too dark. With little heart she clambered up and pushed open the hatch. Immediately a blast of cold wind lifted her hair skywards. She shoved the cap on and yelled for Joseph.

A mug of tea and a ham and lettuce sandwich made with two hunks of wholemeal bread was waiting for her in the cockpit. As she tore into it and swallowed the hot liquid she experienced such a rush of warmth in her stomach that it bordered on bliss.

She glanced up at the mainsail which had been reefed.

'Don't worry, we're well snugged down,' said Joseph,

noticing. 'We've avoided having too much sail in case we can't handle it. We're playing safe, even though it'll take us longer.'

'A hell of a sight longer,' added Ted, and he gave Joseph a grin.

Joseph was beaming.

Tessa gasped at them amazed. They actually looked as if they were getting a kick out of it! How could being tossed around in this cockpit in a biting wind, and being soaked by spray when you were least expecting it, how could they possibly find it enjoyable?

Joseph was holding a chart. He folded it to stop it flapping.

'See this, Tessa,' he said, jabbing at it, 'these are the shipping lanes. We've got to avoid them. It can be as busy out here as rush–hour on the M1.'

She stared at him in disbelief.

'Look!' he said, pointing to her left.

She turned and was surprised to find lights dotted all over the place. He picked up a small round black object with a cord attached to it from the shelf under the doghouse. It looked like a miniature car tyre filled with glass. He hung it round his neck, held it horizontally and peered through a small opening at the side.

'What are you doing?' she asked.

'Taking a compass bearing of that,' he said, glancing over her shoulder.

She looked to where he was peering and screamed. Looming towards them in the dusk like a moving mountain was a monstrous oil-tanker.

'We're going to collide!' she shrieked. 'We'll be crushed!'

'No we won't,' said Joseph calmly. 'Here, come and look through this,' and he hung the compass round her neck.

Tessa drew it slowly up to her eyes.

3

Four hours later she was staring bleakly into the inky darkness as the boat slipped behind high black waves. As it rose she could make out a long line of tiny lights in the distance.

Ted was at the helm. Joseph was below. She heard him coming back up the steps.

'Is he all right?' she asked anxiously.

'His pulse feels regular.'

'Did he take the tea?' asked Ted.

Joseph shook his head.

'But he must be so dehydrated,' Ted exclaimed. 'He's brought up everything he's swallowed.'

'He's sleeping like a baby,' said Joseph. 'If he wasn't, then I'd agree with you and send up a flare.'

'What's a flare?' Tessa asked.

'A red rocket. The coastguards look out for them in case people need help.' He turned to Ted. 'I'm sure he'll survive.'

Ted nodded silently. Joseph came and leaned on the coaming next to her.

'Hastings,' he commented, when the lights came back into view.

'And those?' she asked, pointing out to sea.

'Fishing boats.'

As the boat dipped again and the dark waves obliterated them from sight, Tessa raised the hood of her oilskin. Her ears were still aching from the wind. The boat rose again.

'Any of those Mars bars left?' she heard Ted ask.

'One,' Joseph answered. 'I thought we could split it three ways later when we need some instant energy.'

Three ways, she noted, not four. So they were acting as though she was invisible. She returned to light gazing. She wouldn't ask any more questions. She was obviously still considered a nuisance.

'He's moving!' said Ted suddenly.

They peered down into the dark. Her uncle had stumbled back towards the stove. Probably looking for more pills, Tessa thought. They stared at him motionless, not daring to talk, as though he was a sleep-walker they didn't want to wake suddenly. Transfixed they watched him fumbling with the drawer under the worktop, but instead of taking out pills he drew out the remaining Mars bar, ripped the paper off and frantically bit into it. He was half-way through eating it when he lurched backwards, dropped the remainder of the bar on to the floor, and promptly vomited into his bucket.

Within seconds he was back in his bunk. There was a stunned silence.

'I wouldn't have minded if he'd kept it down,' grumbled Ted.

'What a waste,' sighed Joseph, and he glanced at Tessa. 'Sorry.'

It was then that she realized that the *three* had included her! She shrugged valiantly. 'That's OK,' she said.

'Ever seen a cloud with a silver lining?' he asked.

She smiled. 'No.' Was he trying to tell her there was more chocolate somewhere else?

'Look up and you will.'

She glanced up at the sky and gave an involuntary gasp. Underneath the clouds was a silvery glow.

'What makes it look like that?'

'The moon's behind it. It's beautiful, isn't it?'

She nodded. It was.

Suddenly the boat pitched violently, throwing her back into the side of the cockpit. She gripped the coaming and was about to look up at the sky again when she spotted a shadowy head emerge from the sea.

'There's a dead body in the water!' she shrieked.

'Where?' yelled Ted from above.

She pointed wildly at it. He gave a short laugh.

'It's a dolphin!'

She squinted and looked again. He was right.

The two men leaned excitedly over the coaming.

'Extraordinary!' cried Joseph.

The dark shape bobbed up and down a few times by the port bow and then disappeared.

'I wonder if it'll stay with us,' said Ted.

'I've never seen a dolphin outside a zoo before!' Tessa exclaimed.

'Me neither,' added Joseph.

They peered out into the night, trying to catch sight of it again.

Tessa gave a yawn.

'Joseph,' said Ted suddenly, 'we ought to have watches.'

'We can't take naps with Nick ill,' Joseph began, 'although . . .' And he glanced at Tessa. 'Think you could take the helm while one of us deals with the sail on a tack? Being a cutter she needs two people to handle her.'

Flattered, Tessa nodded.

'She'll need sleep too,' said Ted.

'Of course. We can take it in turns.'

Joseph let her use his sleeping-bag on the top bunk, opposite the bunk where her uncle slept. There was so little space that she had to wriggle into it on her back. She took off Joseph's Guernsey and made herself a pillow with it. It was strange lying down next to a porthole and seeing nothing but sea beside her.

She was convinced she wouldn't be able to fall asleep – conditions at sea made everything feel too damp – but as soon as she began to feel warm she was dragged instantly into unconsciousness.

Occasionally she awoke to feel the cool breeze from the open hatch on the cabin roof drifting across her face. She tried to roll over on to her side but she ached too much to move. Once when she woke she discovered that a blanket had been tucked round her and there was a soft light in the cabin. She raised her head to see where it was coming from. Joseph was leaning over the chart table, an old woolly hat on, writing in a log-book. The light was coming from a small oil-lamp swinging from the hook by his head.

It was much later when she woke properly. She peered out of the porthole only to find the dark waves still crashing against the glass.

She wriggled out of the sleeping-bag and lowered herself over the side into her canvas shoes. Shivering, she drew the warm Guernsey back over her head. She glanced over at her uncle and observed the rise and fall of his chest. He was still alive. Grabbing the cap and oil-skins she staggered towards the cockpit, reaching out with her free hand for anything solid she could take hold of to support her.

As soon as she stepped out of the cabin, the cold wind socked her with such force it sent her reeling. Joseph was at the helm, standing on the deck. Ted was taking a bearing.

'What time is it?' she asked.

'Half-past threeish,' said Ted.

'I'm ready to help if one of you wants a sleep.'

'Not me,' said Ted.

'I wouldn't mind a kip,' said Joseph.

Ted took over at the helm and Joseph went below. Tessa hurriedly dragged on her oilskins and stuck her cap on. Ted asked her to look out for a particular light. She stared intently into the darkness, her fingers frozen as she gripped the coaming.

Though noisy and awe-inspiring, the waves had a peaceful quality to them. Each time they slapped the boat, an icy spray would smack her in the face, but it was pointless to protest and soon she found herself accepting having soaked oilskins, a damp cap and water dripping from her numbed nose. For the first time in months, gazing out at the unending sea, her homework faded into insignificance.

She was surprised to see Joseph step out of the cabin.

'Couldn't you sleep?' she asked.

'I only needed a quick snooze. I feel much better now. Fancy some tea?'

Tessa beamed. 'Yes, please!'

It was later, while warming her hands round her mug that she was suddenly dazzled by a brilliant white light sweeping across the sea. Behind the dim glow which followed it, she could see soaring chalky-white cliffs. It was a spectacular sight. Within seconds the light swept across the waves again and the cliffs came back into view.

'Beachy Head,' said Joseph.

'Isn't that near Newhaven?'

'Yes and no. It's about eight miles.'

'But eight miles is close.'

'In a car it is, not out at sea, and not when you're having to tack as slowly as we are.'

'Why don't we motor-sail?' suggested Ted.

'That's not a bad idea. I'll check the engine hasn't any water in it.'

The engine was fine. As soon as Tessa heard it chug into life, it was all she could do not to sing. She would never have believed that the sound of an old engine could have given her so much pleasure.

The feeling did not last. The engine gave a clunk and then there was silence.

Tessa pressed herself against the back of the cockpit and slid down on to one of the steps. Joseph fiddled with the gearbox and then began lifting up floor-boards and prodding and banging in the bilges. Tessa tried to see what he was doing, but it was too dark.

She listened, her fingers crossed tightly, but aside from the occasional cough, the engine remained ominously quiet.

'I think there must be something caught up in the screw,' he remarked at last.

He dived into the cabin and returned with a boat-hook. Leaning over the coaming he thrust it over the side. Within seconds he gave a loud yell. The boat-hook was being dragged out of his hand. Ted leapt towards him and grabbed it. Tessa instantly jumped up and steadied the tiller. She was surprised at how confident and at home she felt. At school and at home she was always being told how slowly she responded. Now she seemed to move before she thought.

'Thanks,' said Ted when he took it from her.

She noticed they were none too happy.

'We've found out what it is. A huge piece of industrial plastic,' Joseph explained. 'There's no way we can sort it out until we're moored.'

'You mean we can't use the engine?' Tessa exclaimed.

'No. So it's sailing all the way. At least the tide will be washing us in once we reach Newhaven.'

'I don't think we'd better mention this to Nick,' said Ted quietly.

They reached Newhaven at midday. It had been sunny all morning, but out at sea the warmth failed to penetrate Tessa's frozen limbs. It wasn't till they entered the channel that Tessa grew so hot that she had to take off her oilskins.

Sailing slowly down it, dwarfed on either side by the seventy-feet-high pierheads, Tessa shaded her eyes and looked upwards for signs of life, but it was useless. The colossal walls of steel and timber were twice the height of the mast and only if she was lucky did she catch sight of someone's head.

As they dawdled along, all sails up, whilst countless vessels motored speedily past them, Tessa gazed mesmerized at the mass of glistening seaweed hanging like slapping ribbons from the black, rust-stained bulks. Beneath the seaweed, thousands of sharp barnacles were stuck like a collage of giant shells against it.

The mainsail hardly moved. They were so sheltered they were lucky to get breeze-power let alone wind-power. Twice they lost steerage completely. It was as if they had no rudder. No matter what Ted and Joseph tried to do, the boat swung completely out of their control and began to point out to sea. People from passing vessels screamed out at them from their cockpits as Joseph and Ted repeatedly yelled back, 'We've no engine!'

While Joseph helmed, she and Ted would stand on deck with boat-hooks ready to fend off if they were thrown too close to a pierhead or other boats. Then a gust would catch the sails and they would be in control again.

As soon as they reached the marina the mainsail was dropped and Joseph leapt with a rope across a massive gap on to the jetty. The only way the boat could be manoeuvred into a berth was for him to walk round the moored boats and pull theirs into a space between two others. Tessa could not bear to look. Having come this far she couldn't take any more disasters. She turned her back and hastily busied herself tying the mainsail to the boom.

Even after they had found a berth and she had glimpsed Joseph out of the corner of her eye readjusting the ropes which tied them to the catwalk, Tessa still could not bring herself to watch. It wasn't till after he and Ted had helped with the remainder of the mainsail that she turned and stared at the catwalk in disbelief. After being at sea for over twenty-four hours she still couldn't believe they had made it. She surveyed the marina. Hundreds of metal masts glinted in the sunlight and the air was filled with a cacophony of jingling sounds like lots of little chinese bells ringing. She had never heard anything so lovely.

Joseph didn't seem to be taking much notice of them. He was too busy tying the old tyres back over the side.

'What's that noise?' she asked.

'The halyards.'

'What are they?'

'The ropes we pull the sails up with. If they're not tied down, the breeze catches them and they jangle. Haven't you ever heard them before?'

'No. The only boats I've been around are at indoor boat shows. There's no breeze there.'

'Like it?'

She smiled. 'Yes.'

As she gazed at all the gleaming polished boats she was surprised to discover that she didn't envy them. In fact they didn't seem like real boats at all, more like floating caravans. She noticed a few people appearing in their cockpits and staring in their direction and she found herself feeling a mixture of amusement and pride. The cutter was the only boat in sight which had a wooden mast. It might be an ancient tub, she thought, but it had looked after them in wild seas and fierce winds and brought them home.

'Tessa!'

She turned.

'Ted and I are going to a café we know to have breakfast. Coming?'

'I haven't any money.'

'On us.'

'Yes, please. I'm starving. But what about my uncle?'

'He's still breathing steadily. We'll leave a note and tell him where we are in case he wakes.'

As she clambered off the boat and on to the catwalk she felt the wooden boards move rapidly under her feet. She leaned quickly to one side to regain her balance.

'I didn't realize this was a floating catwalk,' she said, surprised. 'I thought it was fixed.'

Ted grinned. 'It is.'

'But it's moving. I can feel it tipping me over.'

'No it isn't.' Joseph laughed. 'You've found your sea-legs, that's all. If you think this is moving, wait till you sit at a table and try to eat.'

Joseph was right. Sitting in the café, trying to tuck

into a cooked breakfast was like trying to play chess on deck in a gale-force wind. Every time she glanced down at her eggs and bacon, the table rose up and then tipped to one side. Once they had finished eating she couldn't wait to get back on to the boat.

Her uncle was still sleeping deeply when they staggered back into the cabin. Speechless with tiredness, they gave him a cursory glance before crawling swiftly into their sleeping-bags, except for Joseph who wrapped a blanket round himself in the bunk underneath Tessa. Ted lay on the top bunk opposite.

It was some time later that she was woken out of a deep sleep by voices on the catwalk. Somebody was recounting one of his sailing adventures. She listened for a moment before closing her eyes.

'We were pitching so violently,' she heard him say, 'it wrenched out the wooden shoe. Next thing we knew the anchor had gone overboard and the chain was rushing after it.'

Poor bloke, thought Tessa, drowsily, knowing what he must have been through.

'Oh no!' said another male voice. 'What the hell did you do?'

Tessa had hardly fallen back to sleep again when the voices pulled her back into consciousness.

'Too risky returning to Rye,' the man continued, 'so we kept sailing through the night against tremendous winds.'

Tessa rolled over sleepily and peered through the porthole. A pair of yellow boots was pacing up and down the catwalk. She guessed they belonged to the story-teller.

'That must have been frightening,' commented another member of his audience.

The man laughed. 'It was. Let's face it, anyone who says they're not frightened in those circumstances must be lying.'

Tessa yawned and attempted to get back to sleep, but as the man on the catwalk continued to give a graphic account of his trip from Rye to Newhaven, Tessa began to find the story vaguely familiar. She leaned over the edge of her bunk and looked down.

Her uncle's bunk was empty.

'I don't believe it!' she muttered, amazed.

Looking up she discovered that Ted was also awake. He was beaming. From underneath her bunk there was an explosion of laughter.

'How can you?' she protested. 'He didn't lift a finger and there he is out there acting as if he sailed this boat single-handed. Aren't you going to stop him?'

Joseph poked his head out, a broad smile on his face.

'He has to have some pleasures from sailing,' he said.

'But he's telling lies!' And then she stopped. 'Wait a minute. Has he done this before?'

'Sort of,' said Joseph. 'It's just that he likes the idea of sailing and all the things associated with it, but if the water isn't as still as a mill-pond, he's seasick.'

'Seasick! You mean that illness was just seasickness?'

'Seasickness can be very debilitating.'

'Seasick!' she spluttered.

'Nelson used to get seasick,' said Ted.

'You're joking! Really?'

Joseph nodded.

'Well he's not going to get away with it this time. The stories he's told my family. Ooh I'm so cross!' And she threw herself on to her back and scowled.

'And just as we were approaching Newhaven,' she heard her uncle say, 'the engine stopped.'

'Oh. Bad luck,' chorused his listeners.

'Seawater got inside?' asked one.

'No. Some industrial plastic caught up in the screw. Nearly took the boat-hook. And us.'

This was greeted with laughter.

'You wait,' muttered Tessa through gritted teeth. She closed her eyes and willed his voice into oblivion. 'You'll get your come-uppance later.'

As she lay there, rehearsing all the insults she was going to hurl at him, she was suddenly aware again of the jangling halyards in the marina. She touched the beams above her head and then turned to look at the tiny bookcase behind her. It was filled with old paperbacks. She gazed at the chronometer with its bronze surround on the wall beside the door to the Heads and at the hatch and at all the old creaking wood which surrounded her, and she knew she would never betray her uncle to her parents. If she did, they would be so horrified they would never let her go sailing with him again. In that moment she realized she was hooked, that her life would never be the same again. The sea hadn't just entered her legs, it had seeped into her bloodstream. She glanced at Ted. He was asleep.

'Joseph,' she said quietly.

'Mm?'

'I've decided not to say anything after all.'

'I thought you'd change your mind. Think you'd like to come again?'

'Can I?'

He laughed. 'Of course.'

She took a last look through the porthole. Her uncle's boots were still marching up and down the catwalk and he was still expounding.

'But I'll never ever wear yellow wellies,' she said

with determination. 'I'll save up for blue ones instead.' And with that she closed her eyes and allowed the cutter to rock her creakily back to sleep.